She Opened Her Eyes....

"Trace?"

His name spoken in Cindy's husky voice sent a primitive shiver of sensation down Trace's spine.

"I'm right here, princess."

She turned toward the sound and thought she was still dreaming. "But I'm not a princess," Cindy said, her voice soft, her eyes openly approving of everything she saw in the man who stood before her.

"You are to me," Trace said simply. Green eyes searched Cindy's face, hardly able to believe the perfection he saw. As he bent down to brush his lips over her soft mouth, he whispered, "You're too beautiful for me, princess. Will you stay with me, even though I'm not a prince?"

He smelled of mist and forest and passion. "You're a man," she said huskily. "More man than I've ever known. That's all I care about." A delicate shiver took her as her lips pressed against his shoulder. "And if I can't have you soon, I'll die...."

Dear Reader:

Welcome! You hold in your hand a Silhouette Desire—your ticket to a whole new world of reading pleasure.

A Silhouette Desire is a sensuous, contemporary romance about passions, problems and the ultimate power of love. It is about today's woman—intelligent, successful, giving—but it is also the story of a romance between two people who are strong enough to follow their own individual paths, yet strong enough to compromise, as well.

These books are written by, for and about every woman that you are—wife, mother, sister, lover, daughter, career woman. A Silhouette Desire heroine must face the same challenges, achieve the same successes, in her story as you do in your own life.

The Silhouette reader is not afraid to enjoy herself. She knows when to take things seriously and when to indulge in a fantasy world. With six books a month, Silhouette Desire strives to meet her many moods, but each book is always a compelling love story.

Make a commitment to romance—go wild with Silhouette Desire!

Best,

Isabel Swift
Senior Editor & Editorial Coordinator

ELIZABETH LOWELL
Dark Fire

Silhouette Desire

Published by Silhouette Books New York

America's Publisher of Contemporary Romance

SILHOUETTE BOOKS
300 East 42nd St., New York, N.Y. 10017

ISBN: 0-373-05462-9

First Silhouette Books printing November 1988

Printed in the U.S.A.

ELIZABETH LOWELL

is a pseudonym for Ann Maxwell, who also writes with her husband under the name of A. E. Maxwell. Her novels range from science fiction to historical fiction and from romance to the sometimes gritty reality of modern suspense. All of her novels share a common theme—the power and beauty of love.

Prologue

———

"You want me to do *what*?" Trace Rawlings asked, raising dark eyebrows.

The man called Invers sighed and rubbed his palm over his thinning hair. "You heard me the first time."

"I've been back in Quito for less than an hour," Trace pointed out. "That damned Polish orchid hunter you sicced on me was the genuine article. He was after orchids, period, and he would have taken on hell with a bucket of water to get to them."

Invers tried to look sympathetic. He failed. He needed Trace too badly to be diverted by something as useless as compassion.

Trace swore under his breath and glared at the small passport photo Invers had given to him. A woman's face stared back at him. Cynthia Edwinna Ryan McCall had black hair, midnight eyes, skin as fine as expensive porcelain, a remote expression and a father who could make highly placed American embassy officials sweat bullets.

"Hell," Trace muttered. He looked up, pinning Invers with a jungle-green glance. "After this, we're even."

Invers let out a rushing breath. "We'll be better than even, Trace. I won't forget this, believe me."

Trace grunted.

"She'll land in a few minutes, so we'll have to be quick. The passport is issued in the name of Cynthia Ryan. She won't tell anyone who she really is. Also, she doesn't know that her father has been in contact with us."

"Does it matter?"

Invers rubbed his palm over his head again, a sign of his unhappiness. Silently he wondered just how much of the story he could tell Trace before the other man would throw up his hands and back out. To anyone who didn't know Big Eddy, the whole story would sound preposterous. To anyone who did know him, the whole story would sound like what it was: preposterous but all too true.

"You ever meet Big Eddy McCall when you were in the States?" Invers asked cautiously.

"No."

"Um. Well. Ms. Ryan doesn't get along with her father. Not surprising. Nobody really *gets* along with Big Eddy. You *go* along with him or you go under. Nothing personal, you understand. That's just the way he is. A real steamroller."

Trace grunted again. "What about her?"

"Ms. Ryan? Oh, she must be at least as stubborn as he is. More stubborn in some ways. Every man her father has picked out for her has been thrown back in his face. He's finally given up on marrying her off." Invers paused as though struck by a new thought. "By God, that's quite an accomplishment. I think she might be the first human being ever to say no to Big Eddy and make it stick."

"So?"

Invers rubbed his head again as he gave Trace a sideways glance. Everything Invers had said so far was technically true. Big Eddy had given up on marriage for his daughter. He had not, however, given up on the idea of grandchildren. He wanted an Edward Ryan McCall IV to be born as soon as possible. One of his sons had produced a grandchild. That wasn't enough. Big Eddy wanted about a dozen other grandkids as backup for life's nasty little surprises. That was where his daughter came in. Big Eddy had finally figured out that a woman didn't have to be married in order to have children.

Invers didn't think Trace was ready to hear about that part of Big Eddy's proposed deal. In fact, Invers doubted if Trace would ever be ready to stand at stud for Big Eddy, much less to find out that it had been Raul's idea in the first place. It was the better—indeed the only—part of valor to tell half-truths to Trace and to let Big Eddy believe what he wanted to believe about the man he had ordered Invers to hire. And never to mention Raul at all.

"Um. Well. Big Eddy's daughter goes by the name of Cindy Ryan and is in business with a woman called Susan Parker. That's where you come in."

Trace arched his eyebrows again. It wasn't like Invers to loop around a subject eight times before getting to the point.

"Ms. Parker comes to Quito several times a year to buy cloth," Invers continued. "This time her native buyer didn't show up, so she hopped a bus over the Andes to go looking for him."

"Did she find him?"

"No. She won't, either," Invers added with uncharacteristic bluntness. "When he wasn't buying cloth he was smuggling emeralds out of Colombia. He stiffed one of his connections and hasn't been heard from since."

Trace shrugged. "It happens."

"Yes. Well. Ms. Parker hasn't been heard from for ten days, either. Not officially, that is."

Green eyes focused on Invers with startling intensity. "And unofficially?"

"Unofficially she is the pampered guest of *Señor* Rau Almeda," Invers said. "*Señor* Almeda would like her to remain for a while longer. That's why his shortwave radio are all on the fritz."

Trace hissed an obscenity that Invers chose not to hear.

"From all indications, Ms. Parker isn't burning down the house trying to leave," Invers said.

The left corner of Trace's mouth kicked up slightly. Raul was a good friend as well as a connoisseur of elegant women. Raul was also very well connected to the government of Ecuador, which was why Invers looked so unhappy at the thought of displeasing him.

"So what's the problem?" Trace asked. "Is Ms. Parker's family worried about her?"

"She has no family, but apparently she's rather close to Ms. Ryan, who is flying to Ecuador to find out what happened to her partner."

"I still don't see the problem. Just tell Big Eddy's daughter that her friend is shacked up with every woman's dream lover."

"I suggested a similar solution to *Señor* Almeda."

"Raul didn't go for it?"

"No. He can be rather, um..."

"Autocratic," Trace said flatly. "He was born too late. He should have been an emperor."

Invers, being a diplomat, chose not to point out that Raul was descended from French, Spanish and Inca royalty, and ruled his immense land holdings like the tyrants his ancestors had been. A benevolent tyrant, granted, but a tyrant nonetheless.

"In any case," Invers said smoothly, "we all want to avoid any suggestion of an, um, incident. We can't have Ms. Ryan running around raising an embarrassing hue and cr for Ms. Parker. If we tell Ms. Ryan that Ms. Parker is quit happy on the Almeda *hacienda*, Ms. Ryan will want to tal to her. Then we'll have to tell her that the radio isn't func tioning at the moment and won't be functioning in the near future. I don't think Big Eddy's daughter will find that explanation, um, acceptable.''

Eyes closed, Trace went over all that Invers had said. And more importantly, all that he had not said.

''You're quite certain that Raul's latest captive is a happy captive?'' Trace asked, focusing on Invers with an intensity that made the other man long to be elsewhere.

''As of five days ago, yes.''

''Do you have any indication that Ms. Parker or Ms. Ryan are involved in smuggling of any kind?''

''No, thank God,'' Invers said fervently.

''Then what is it, precisely, that you want me to do?''

''Allow Ms. Ryan to hire you to 'find' her friend. Take your time getting to the Almeda *hacienda*, and—''

''How long?'' Trace interrupted.

''Four or five days. A week at most. *Señor* Almeda isn't known for the duration of his, um, enthusiasms.''

Trace smiled slightly but said only, ''Stalling shouldn't be a problem. That early storm made a mess of the mountain roads.''

''It disrupted communications, too,'' Invers added without missing a beat. ''Be sure to point that out to Ms. Ryan.''

''No problem. Hell, it's the simple truth.''

''There is no such thing as a simple truth,'' Invers muttered beneath his breath.

Trace smiled rather grimly. ''Anything else?''

''Don't reveal that you know Ms. Ryan is Big Eddy McCall's daughter. And be very, very certain that Ms. Ryan doesn't know you have been hired by her father. Otherwise she'll walk out on you and try to hire another guide. That would make things exceptionally, um, difficult for the embassy.''

''Have I been hired by Big Eddy? I thought I was just doing you a favor.''

Smiling blandly, Invers offered Trace one-half of a very complex truth. "Big Eddy requested of the embassy that we hire the best man in Ecuador to guide and protect his daughter while she's here. She would, after all, make a tempting kidnap target. You'll be paid one thousand American dollars a day for your, um, efforts."

Trace's green eyes narrowed. "That seems excessive."

"Big Eddy is excessively rich. Think of it as combat pay," Invers added, smiling thinly.

"Are you really expecting someone to grab her?"

"No. But face it, Trace. I'm not sending you on a picnic. Any woman who can stand up to Big Eddy could teach stubborn to a Missouri mule."

"I'm hardly known as a pushover," Trace pointed out.

"Yes. I am well aware of that fact."

Invers smiled and silently wished that he could go along with Trace and Cindy Ryan. It would be worth considerable inconvenience to find out who taught stubborn to whom.

One

Good work, Invers. It saves a lot of wear and tear on the hunter when the prey walks right into the trap, Trace thought sardonically as he watched the tall, raven-haired woman weaving through the smoky bar toward him.

At that moment Trace was ready to accept any break Lady Luck was passing out. He had left Invers less than twenty minutes before. No time to shower, shave, change clothes or do anything else in the way of recovery from the past six weeks of trying to keep J. Ivar Polanski, orchid collector extraordinaire, from killing himself or someone else while pursuing living baubles to adorn spoiled rich women such as the one crossing the crowded room right now.

Not that Cindy Ryan needed any decoration, Trace decided as she came a bit closer. The face-only photograph hadn't done her justice. She had the kind of figure that made a man... restless.

"Mr. Rawlings? I'm Cynthia Ryan."

The voice was a husky contralto that made every one of Trace's masculine nerve endings stir. His physical response irritated him. So instead of responding immediately, he sipped at the fine Scotch that the waitress had put in front of him a few moments earlier. Without saying a word he let the smoky, intimate taste of the liquor expand through him like a kiss from the kind of woman he had always wanted and never found. Only after the taste on his tongue had dissipated to a shimmering echo of heat did he look up.

At that moment Cindy found herself hoping she was mistaken and that this man was not Trace Rawlings. It was all she could do not to step backward when his cool green eyes focused on her. The man lounging at the small table with his long legs stretched in front of him wasn't what she had expected to hire. She couldn't believe that this man with his stained khaki bush clothes, scarred boots and a dark, three-day stubble on his heavy jaw, was the guide the American embassy had enthusiastically recommended that she hire. Could this be the bilingual backcountry genius who had no peer in Quito, Ecuador or anywhere else up and down the South American Andes?

"Trace Rawlings?" Cindy repeated, knowing her voice was too husky, too skeptical, and unable to do anything about it. The man was frankly unnerving. He radiated the kind of relaxed, clearly undomesticated presence that people associated with cats stretched out in a patch of sunlight. Big cats. Black jaguars, for instance. Dangerously handsome, dangerously powerful, dangerously sleek, dangerously... *dangerous*.

"That's me."

Trace's voice was a perfect match for his appearance. The resonances were deep, predatory and compelling. Nerve endings Cindy didn't know she had stirred and shivered in dark response.

"Do you have any identification?" Cindy asked finally, frowning as she looked Trace over once more.

Her opinion hadn't changed since her first glance at him. There was nothing reassuring about Trace Rawlings, and Cindy very much needed reassurance right now. Susan had been missing for ten days, and Susan, whatever her quirks, was not the type to vanish without leaving so much as a note for her friend.

Trace felt his irritation turn into a razor edge of anger at the dubious looks he kept getting from Big Eddy's snooty daughter. Coolly Trace gave Cindy precisely the kind of once-over she had just given him.

"ID?" he asked softly. "Sure thing." He turned and called to the bartender in machine-gun Spanish and instantly was answered in the same way. "Anything else?" Trace asked indifferently, reaching for the Scotch once more.

"I beg your pardon?"

Someday, you'll do just that, princess—and mean it, Trace thought with a surge of purely masculine emotion as he sipped the aromatic golden liquor. *Snotty rich girls who go slumming in the wrong places tend to get men knifed in back alleys.* And beneath that thought was another: *God, if Cindy's partner is half as sexy, no wonder Raul wanted to sabotage the radio, lock all the doors and drop the keys into the nearest sacred well.*

"You wanted ID. Paco vouched for me," Trace said carelessly. "We've known each other for years."

"But I don't understand Spanish."

Trace shrugged. "Tough taco, princess. It's the language of the day around here."

Cindy's black eyes narrowed. When Trace focused his attention once more on his Scotch, she fought a sudden, sharp struggle with her temper. Normally she would have been the first to find humor in the situation confronting her, but nothing was normal for her right now. She was tired, had a screaming headache from Quito's ten thousand feet of altitude and was worried about Susan.

In no way did Cindy feel like catering to the irrational male whims of a lean, dark, down-at-the-heels American who had gone native.

"Well, Tarzan, put this in your taco," Cindy drawled. "Invers at the embassy told me that a man called Trace Rawlings has been known to hire himself out . . . if the price is right. So I guess I'll just have to start naming figures. When the price is right, Trace Rawlings will stand up and be counted."

Only the fact that Cindy had been raised by a steamroller disguised as a father, and had an older brother whose temper was frankly formidable, gave her the courage not to turn and run when Trace looked up at her. There was a long silence while she returned him stare for glare.

Slowly Trace smiled.

Cindy felt tiny shivers chase up and down her spine. If she had believed she could outrun Trace, she would have sprinted for the door right then. But she knew she couldn't outrun him, so she didn't even try. Trace was acclimatized to Quito's staggering altitude, but lack of oxygen would bring her down before she had taken thirty steps. There was no choice for her now but to dig in right where she was and brazen it out the way she had always done with her father.

Besides, Susan was somewhere out in the wilds alone, and this was the wild man who could find her.

"One hundred dollars a day," Cindy said, her voice too husky, almost breathless.

Trace's cold green eyes looked Cindy over again in a very leisurely manner, admiring all the velvet curves and alluring shadows, noting with a kind of distant surprise that she had made no effort to enhance or even to announce the feminine bounty beneath her clothes. The off-white jumpsuit she wore was loose and wrinkled. The belt around her waist could have been tightened several more notches without cutting into tender flesh. She wore flat sandals rather than heels, which would have emphasized the sway of her shapely hips. Her toenails were bare of polish. So were her fingers. If she wore makeup, it didn't show in the bar's dim light.

Maybe that's why Big Eddy keeps picking out men for her—she's so rich she's never bothered to learn all the little tricks and traps poor girls use to get men interested.

"Two hundred."

Trace flicked another disparaging glance over Cindy and went back to his Scotch. *The most important thing I'll teach her is that there are some things money can't buy—and Trace Rawlings is right at the top of the list.*

"Three hundred."

Angrily Trace wished that he had told Invers to go spit up a rope. But Trace hadn't been that smart. Instead he had promised to keep an eye on Big Eddy's obviously spoiled daughter. In order to do that Trace had to appear to be hired by her...which meant she would think she had bought him.

Combat pay. And I'll earn every nickel of it.

Trace shrugged again. His pride could take it. He had suffered far worse blows and survived. And he owed Invers.

"Four hundred."

Trace stretched, bringing his long arms and large hands high over his head. Cindy measured his size and length and realized with a sudden curious weakness in her knees that she was within his reach.

"Five hundred," she said in a rush.

"Princess, you just hired yourself a guide."

Cindy looked at Trace and wondered how Red Riding Hood would have felt if she had hired the Big Bad Wolf to guide her through the terrors and traps of the forest.

She would have felt the way I do now. Scared!

"All right." Cindy took a deep breath, telling herself she was relieved to have hired a guide, wishing she believed it. "My friend and business partner, Susan Parker, came to Quito to buy native weavings. But she doesn't speak Spanish so she has a native buyer who meets her in Quito and turns over all the cloth from the various native villages on his circuit. You see, we have clothing boutiques on both coasts of the U.S., and Susan is a designer, and we . . . never mind, that's not important," Cindy said, realizing that she was babbling but unable to stop completely. Trace was too unnerving. She wanted to run but she couldn't, so the next best thing was to finish hiring the jungle cat, find Susan and get the hell away from those disdainful green eyes.

"Susan arrived in Quito ten days ago," Cindy said quickly. "Pedro, the native buyer, didn't show up. She called me and said she was going to check the villages on Pedro's circuit. That was ten days ago. I haven't heard from her since. She hasn't checked out of the hotel, but she hasn't been in her room since she asked directions to the bus. The clerk wrote them for her in phonetic Spanish so she could say them correctly."

Trace reached for the Scotch. "Bus? Phonetic Spanish?"

"She doesn't drive or speak Spanish. She was born in Manhattan."

Trace grunted. "Let me see if I have this straight." He finished off the Scotch and looked at Cindy with heavy-lidded eyes. "Your friend doesn't speak Spanish, doesn't drive and is somewhere out in the boondocks looking for a native known to her only as 'Pedro.'"

Scarlet stained Cindy's cheekbones. Put that way it made Susan sound as though she had the IQ of a toothbrush. That wasn't the case.

"I assure you, Mr. Rawlings, Susan is an accomplished traveler. She speaks neither Arabic nor Chinese, yet she has traveled extensively—and alone—in the Middle East and China."

Trace grunted. "Then why are you worried about her?"

"She always leaves me an itinerary. When that isn't possible she calls every few days. Never less than once a week. It has been ten days since her last call."

"Maybe she found Pedro or some other native and holed up with him for a little slap and tickle." Trace let his glance rove over Cindy's body again. "It happens, you know."

"Not to me," Cindy retorted instantly.

"But you're not the one who's lost, are you?"

"Mr. Rawlings—"

"Yes, Cindy?" he interrupted.

The casual use of her first name didn't escape Cindy. Trace was flatly stating that he was in control of the situation and she was not.

"For five hundred dollars a day I expect a little less insolence, *Trace*."

"Say it again, princess," he murmured.

"What?" she said scathingly. "Your name?"

"No. Insolence. You put just the right amount of nose into it," Trace added, brushing the nail of his index finger beneath his nose in a mocking gesture. "You learned that at a fancy finishing school, I'll bet. Pity they didn't teach you something useful, like good manners."

Cindy felt another wash of heat over her cheekbones and made a desperate attempt to get a grip on her fraying self-control. She told herself she was feeling emotional because of the altitude, the worry, the lack of sleep... anything but the fact that she hated seeing masculine disdain in Trace's cold green eyes. She closed her own eyes, hoping that the stabbing, screaming pain of her headache would be calmed by darkness.

No such luck.

"Mr. Rawlings, I don't have the time or energy to play word games with you." Cindy opened her eyes. "My friend is missing. I was told you were the best man to find her. I have met your price. Could we just get on with it?"

"Oh, you've got plenty of time to play games," Trace said, signaling for another drink. Against his better judgment he used his right foot to shove out a chair for Cindy. "Sit down before you fall down."

Trace spoke over Cindy's shoulder to the waitress, who was approaching with his Scotch. Cindy understood just enough of the Spanish to be irritated by what he had ordered for her.

"I'm old enough to drink," she said.

"Dumb enough, too, I'll bet."

"Is that the voice of experience speaking?" she asked, looking pointedly at the Scotch Trace had just picked up.

"You'd better believe it, princess."

The whiplash of Trace's voice snapped Cindy's attention back to his face. Not for the first time she realized that he was not a man whose looks inspired a gentle glow of comfort in a woman. Without glancing away from Cindy's pale, strained expression, Trace raised his voice and called out again in rapid Spanish. Two more rounds of Scotch materialized with dazzling speed, accompanied by a warm bottle of Coke.

"Drink up," Trace said, gesturing to the liquor and simultaneously snagging the bottle of Coke in one big hand, taking it out of her reach.

Cindy looked warily at the Scotch. "Why?"

"Right now your head feels like someone buried a hatchet in it, your stomach has a sour disposition and walking across the room is like going up a flight of stairs. It's called altitude sickness. If you want to make it worse, have a shot or two of liquor. Have it on me. The sooner you drink, the sooner you'll know that I *am* experienced in this territory. You aren't. I may be a peon, but you need me, princess. The quicker you get that straight, the better off you'll be."

Cindy sat down and looked away from the jungle-green eyes staring at her, labeling her, dismissing her. The pain in her head doubled suddenly, making her breath catch. The airline flight attendant had warned the passengers that altitude sickness wasn't uncommon for the first few days in Quito. The best advice was to rest as much as possible, eat lightly, drink juices and take aspirin for the headache. If you didn't feel better after a few days, you were supposed to go to a lower elevation.

And stay there.

Sighing, Cindy put her elbows on the table and massaged her temples. "Sorry to disappoint you, Mr. Rawlings. I like my headache just the way it is. No additives necessary. So drink up. My treat." When the silence had stretched to the point of discomfort, she grimaced. "The first village on Susan's list was Popocaxtil. Do you know it?"

"Yes."

"How long will it take us to get there?" Cindy lifted her head and unflinchingly met Trace's green glance. "Don't try to talk me out of going with you. If Susan is hurt or needs help, I want to be there for her."

"Is she your sister?"

"No."

"Your lover?"

Cindy's jaw dropped. She tried to say something but no words came out.

It was Trace's turn to sigh. There went the obvious explanation for the fact that a woman who looked like Cindy—and was rich into the bargain—was neither married nor, if Invers were to be believed, interested in men at all.

"Women have been known to prefer women," Trace pointed out calmly.

"Having met you I'm beginning to understand why!" Cindy pushed the two shot glasses of Scotch away from her with a sweep of her slender hands. "How far is it to Popocaxtil?" she demanded.

"It depends."

"I'm waiting breathlessly. On what does it depend?"

"The weather," Trace said succinctly.

"When I landed an hour ago, the weather was just fine."

"You were lucky. The rainy season is early this year. The area around Popocaxtil had a hell of a storm four or five days ago. Part of the main blacktop road washed out. As for the last fifteen klicks of the dirt road to the village..." Trace shrugged. "It will be two, probably three days before the road will dry out enough to be passable."

"Klicks?"

"Kilometers."

"Oh. Fifteen kilometers is about seven miles, isn't it?"

"Close enough."

"That's not very far."

Trace's very dark eyebrows were deeply arched to begin with. When he raised one of them in a silent show of skepticism, he appeared almost diabolical.

"That depends," he said.

"On the weather?" Cindy retorted.

"You're learning."

"We'll just have to tough out the weather. I can't sit around here waiting for—"

"Princess, I just got back from six weeks of camping out in the lowlands," Trace interrupted. "If you think I'm going to spend the next two days winching my Rover out of bogs instead of relaxing and soaking up some of the joys of civilization while the mountain roads dry out, you're nuts."

"I can't believe I'm hearing this. Susan might be lost and afraid and hurt and all you can think about is having a Scotch?"

"Don't forget a hot shower," Trace suggested softly.

"Why not? You apparently did, along with a shave and clean clothes!" Cindy made a sharp gesture with her hand. "Never mind. There's no sense in appealing to your better nature. I doubt that you have one. Seven hundred a day and we leave right now."

Trace picked up his second Scotch, held the glass against the table light and admired the liquid's fine color. "No."

The refusal was so soft that it took a moment for it to register on Cindy.

"Eight hundred," she said angrily.

"No."

"Nine!"

"Princess, there are some things money can't buy. I'm one of them. If you need my help, ask. Don't wave money."

"Ask? *Ask!* What do you think I've been doing?"

"Demanding or buying."

"Instead of begging?" Cindy suggested icily. "Haven't you learned yet, Tarzan? All begging gets you is sore knees." She pushed away from the table and stood, ignoring the hammer blows of pain in her head. "Fortunately I won't have to wear my knees out on your masculine ego. I don't need you. I'll check out the villages myself."

"How? You don't speak Spanish, much less any of the local Indian dialects."

"Neither does Susan."

"Look where it got her."

"I'm planning on it!"

Trace laughed derisively. "Sure you are." He glanced at Cindy's pallor, at her lips drawn flat with pain and at the fine trembling of her hands. "Go back to your room and lie down, princess. I'll pick you up Thursday morning at your hotel at dawn."

Cindy spun on her heel and walked out, neither looking back at Trace nor aside at any of the interested patrons watching the tall *gringa* stalking away from the bar. She was furious with herself for handling Trace so badly and furious with him for being such an unbending, overweaning s.o.b., and furious with life for putting her in a situation where her father's money—which she would never have touched for any reason less urgent than Susan's disappearance—couldn't even buy a decent guide.

Smiling coolly, Trace watched Cindy leave. He had been rough on her and he knew it, but it had been a cut-and-dried case of self-defense. He had been caught flat-footed by her, his dropped jaw flapping in the wind. Nothing in Invers's briefing or in the picture Trace had been given of Cindy had even hinted at the real woman. Quick, intelligent, vital, with black eyes whose clarity and enigmatic depths challenged a man. And she had something more, something Trace had dreamed about but never found.

Beneath that cool exterior Cindy McCall burned with the kind of passionate, dark fire that a man would kill for. Or die for.

Trace had felt an answering fire licking through his body. It was still there, burning, urging. He ignored it now as he had ignored it in Cindy's presence, knowing that to give in was to hand himself over to his sensuous combatant without a murmur of protest. He wouldn't allow that to happen.

The smile on Trace's lips curled higher as he realized that he was probably the first man ever to say no to Ms. Cynthia Edwinna Ryan McCall. It must have been a salutary learning experience for her. At the very least, in the future she wouldn't look down her nose at Trace Rawlings with such fine disdain. She needed him. It would be a pure pleasure to hear her admit it.

Smiling, Trace sipped at his Scotch.

He was still smiling Thursday morning when he drove over to pick up Cindy, only to discover that she had rented a Jeep and set off down the highway for Popocaxtil on Tuesday.

Two

Cindy stared at the smudged, rumpled map again. If she were right, she was definitely on the road to Popocaxtil. If she were wrong, she was one lost puppy.

She looked dubiously through the cracked windshield at the so-called road, which was a raw gash that wound up and down and sideways across the shoulder of a mountain whose top and bottom were hidden in clouds. The dense forest of the uplands had given way to an equally dense cover of brushy plants. The road had remained the same...awful. She hadn't seen a road sign since yesterday.

The one nice thing was that Cindy's headache had finally gone. She didn't know whether she had become accustomed to the thin air or the road had really dropped more in altitude than it had subsequently gained clawing its way back up the mountain. All she knew for certain was that her headache had departed, and for that blessing she was profoundly grateful.

Again Cindy looked from the map to the road. Hers were the only vehicle tracks to mark the rutted, overgrown track since the last rain.

"I'm not lost," she said aloud, wishing it didn't sound so much like a question.

"You're not lost," she answered herself firmly.

She heard the conversation with herself and muttered, "I'm going crazy."

"No, you're not," she retorted immediately. "You just like to hear English spoken after days of incomprehensible Spanish."

"Really? That makes me feel better. Know something? I like you."

"It's mutual."

"Maybe I *am* going crazy."

"No, you're just stalling. You don't want to go back to wrestling with the Jeep."

"You're right."

The paved road Cindy had started out on had been no treat once Quito's environs had been left behind, but compared to the secondary and tertiary roads she had encountered since then, the paved road had been a miracle of modern engineering. Her whole body ached from fighting the Jeep over the rain-greased road.

Sighing, Cindy leaned forward and turned the ignition key. The engine started immediately, a fact that continued to surprise her each time it occurred. To be diplomatic, the Jeep had an aura of experience about it. To be factual, the Jeep looked as though it had been through the wars, all of them, beginning with the Crimean and progressing right on through Vietnam.

Despite that, the vehicle seemed quite hardy, if Cindy discounted the tires' distressing tendency to flatten at inconvenient moments. Not that any moment would have been truly convenient. The first flat had occurred yesterday, after only a few hours on a detour to bypass a washout on the main paved road. She had barely begun to wrestle with the jack when a boy who looked too young to be out in the world on his own had walked by, seen her distress and stopped to help her.

The language barrier proved to be irrelevant. A flat tire by any other name was still not round. The boy had simply handed his baggage into Cindy's keeping and had proceeded to whisk off the tire, put on the spare and watch with fatalistic good humor as the tire promptly sank onto its own rim. The spare had been as flat as the other one.

The boy had pried both tires off their rims, patched the inner tubes and pumped them up, using tools from the battered box that was bolted in the cargo area of the Jeep. Then he had put all the pieces together again, giving Cindy two good tires. During the entire process she had stood in the cool drizzle and held the boy's precious baggage—a burlap sack containing two monumentally unhappy piglets—and watched what he was doing very carefully. The patching procedure was simple. Find the leak, clean the area to be patched, apply sticky stuff to the patch and the patch to the tire, hang on tight to everything and count to fifty-eight thousand while two piglets achieved operatic heights of despair within the burlap bag.

Even the memory of it made Cindy laugh aloud. She wished she had a picture of herself holding a sack with two bouncing pigs in one hand and an umbrella in the other hand, while rain ran in rivulets from her chin and elbows as she leaned over and braced herself against the Jeep in an effort to keep the boy dry during a sudden shower. But if she had had that picture she would have traded it for the one she really wanted, that of a busload of natives standing in the muck up to their ankles as they argued and gesticulated robustly about the best way to free her Jeep from an entanglement consisting of uninjured but outraged livestock, a pile of kindling that could have filled a church and enough mud to build the Great Wall of China.

Still grinning at the memories, Cindy eased the Jeep from the verge back into the road. And it was *into* rather than *onto* the road. The ruts were twin and sometimes triplicate trenches filled with water. The water looked either brown or gunmetal gray, depending on the angle of the sun through the dispersing clouds.

No matter how hard Cindy tried, it was impossible to keep the Jeep's tires entirely free of the ruts. At least there was a bottom to the ruts, she consoled herself. She wasn't at all certain she could say the same about the puddles of water that lurked in low places along the sides of the road. When there was a side to the road, that is. Sometimes there was nothing but a long, long drop into a valley.

Water was everywhere, trickling from each crease and crevice on the steep mountainside. Early that morning the trickles had been creeks and streams, but the runoff had slowed dramatically as the rains diminished in the highlands. The thought cheered Cindy as much as the sunshine streaming between banks of clouds. Soon it would be actually warm instead of nearly warm. Soon the Jeep's canvas roof would stop drooling water down her left shoulder. Soon she would turn a corner and see a tattered Popocaxtil sunk happily into the mire. There she would be able to find food and water and, best of all, word of Susan Parker.

If this were, indeed, the road to Popocaxtil.

It took every bit of Cindy's concentration to enable her to pick her way over nature's obstacle course at a rate slightly faster than that of a three-legged burro. With every yard she progressed she silently thanked her brother Rye for having forced her to learn unwanted skills. Years ago he had insisted that she learn to drive his rugged ranch road in the Jeep he kept for winter transportation. She would never again tease him about his rustic taste in road surfaces. After her experience in Ecuador she would be able to drive Rye's ranch roads at eighty miles per hour blindfolded.

The Jeep's front tires were grabbed by ruts at the same instant that the wheel was wrenched from Cindy's hand. She downshifted for more power, grinding the gears heartlessly. Rye had neglected to show her the finer points of speed shifting or double clutching, a fact that she regretted now. At the time, however, she had thought it outrageous enough that he had insisted she learn to drive primitive roads in a vehicle that lacked an automatic shift. And then she had had to learn to change a tire in the bargain. She had given Rye a steady line of smart remarks while he tutored her, but the next time she saw him she would gratefully go down on her knees in the ranch yard and kiss his dusty boots in thanks for his foresight.

Crunching and groaning, the Jeep clawed out of the deep ruts. Even on flatter ground, the vehicle wanted to lunge to the right. Cindy found a relatively firm spot, stopped and climbed out to see what was wrong. With a sinking heart she realized that the right front tire was a mere shadow of its former rotund self.

"Damn!"

Swearing at the tire wouldn't get it changed. Nor was Cindy's vocabulary extensive enough to make her feel better. Muttering, she went to the back of the Jeep, unbolted the jack, shoved it under the chassis and started leaning on the jack's lever.

What had taken the boy mere minutes to accomplish took her nearly half an hour. Finally the flat tire rose far enough above the mire for her to be able to reach all the lug nuts holding the wheel in place. She grabbed the lug wrench and leaned. It popped off, nearly sending her face-first into the mud. She put the wrench back over the lug nut and leaned again.

Nothing happened.

Cindy leaned harder and then harder still. She had never considered herself an Amazon, but she couldn't believe that she was too weak to remove a simple lug nut. After all, the boy who had helped her yesterday had been her height and he hadn't had much trouble changing a tire. Finally she jammed the lug wrench in place, held onto the Jeep, and jumped onto one arm of the cross-shaped tool, using the weight of her whole body to force the nut to turn.

Five jumps later she managed to loosen the first lug nut. The rest of them weren't as easy. By the time Cindy had dragged the wheel off, rolled it to the back of the Jeep, swapped it for the spare and gotten the spare screwed into its new home to the best of her ability, she was dirty, thirsty, hungry and exhausted. After she put away the tools she sluiced off the worst of her dirt in a rain puddle. The cool, murky water tempted her almost unendurably.

"Don't be an idiot," Cindy told herself as she licked dry lips and wiped her hands on her dirty jeans. "All you need to really make your day is the local version of Montezuma's revenge."

Wearily Cindy pulled herself into the Jeep's rump-sprung seat, started the engine and crept forward, praying that no other tire would flatten. She wasn't going to take time to patch the ruined inner tube right now. In truth, she was afraid that she wouldn't be able to pry the tire off the wheel rim, much less put it back together again.

The next hour was uneventful. Then Cindy came to a steep curve where the road had a pronounced outward slant toward the valley, which was a breathtaking two thousand sheer feet below on the right. Suddenly all four wheels began to spin as the Jeep lost traction in the greasy mud and began to slide sideways inch by inch toward the drop-off. She clung to the wheel and fed gas gently, wondering if forward momentum would get her past the slippery spot before gravity pulled the Jeep into the abyss. Just as she reached for the door handle to jump out, one front wheel finally found good traction and pulled her up and around the dangerous curve.

Over the shoulder of the mountain a long, narrow valley opened up. The surrounding forest had been cut or burned fairly recently, giving the valley floor a ragged, mottled look. Only very small trees and modest bushes grew along the road. There wasn't a drop-off or a curve in sight. After what Cindy had been through, the road looked beautiful.

"Hang on, Susan, wherever you are. I'm coming. Not fast, but I'm coming."

Feeling much more cheerful, Cindy drove down the gentle incline into the valley...and sank right up to her bumpers in mud.

"Gracias," called the man to Trace.

As Trace waved in acknowledgement, the man gunned his rattletrap truck, lifted a rooster tail of dirt into the air and shot around a muddy spot where the main road had washed out. Trace wound the forward winch cable he had used to free the man's truck and climbed back into the big, battered Land Rover. He had covered the distance from Quito to this point in record time, despite the washouts, and every inch of the way he had wondered if he were on a wild-goose chase.

Even after Trace had seen a place on a washout detour where a vehicle had pulled over to change a flat, he hadn't been convinced that the small footprints in the mud had belonged to Cindy. A woman, yes. The disdainful princess? Maybe, but not very damned likely.

Trace hadn't really believed that Cindy had set off alone for Popocaxtil until he had turned off the main road onto the dirt road. At a tiny village where he had stopped for food and water, he had heard the epic of a bus, a Jeep, a mountain of kindling, assorted livestock—and *una Americana muy hermosa* who had black hair, a warm smile and no Spanish to speak of.

Trace hadn't seen Cindy smile, but he doubted that there was more than one beautiful American woman who was traveling the backcountry alone in a Jeep, asking in fractured Spanish along the way for a village called Popocaxtil.

Certainly someone had recently been along the dirt track he was driving. That someone was getting a cram course in four-wheel skills, if the abundance of wallow and skid marks were any indication. At first the Jeep had hit all the bad spots in the road as though it were guided by a perverse sort of radar. As the kilometers went by, Cindy—presuming it was, indeed, Cindy who was steering the Jeep—had learned how to keep the vehicle from getting high-centered between the ruts. She had also learned that the rut-puddle you know is a lot safer than the puddle at the side of the road. Presumably she had also learned to feed gas evenly and firmly in the boggy spots to prevent digging in or fishtailing all over the place.

Now, if only it would rain.

With the cynical eyes of a man who has found answers to questions most people would rather not even ask, Trace measured the clouds. If it didn't rain before sunset he would be surprised. If it did rain, it wouldn't amount to much.

Too bad. A good rain would wash her right out of the game and into my arms.

The phrasing of his own thought made Trace's mouth flatten into a hard line. He had spent two very restless nights thinking about Cindy Ryan's cool intelligence and taut, warm curves. The combination fascinated him even as it challenged him. It also irritated him unreasonably. He was old enough to know his own mind and body very well, but the depth of his response to the lush Ms. Ryan was something new.

And the jungle had taught Trace that new was a synonym for dangerous.

Frowning, he drove on. A few minutes later the road divided. There were no signs to mark towns or directions. The main dirt road went to the left. The fresh tracks he was following went to the right. In the distance, the road began snaking up the steep side of a mountain.

"She must have been born under a lucky star," he muttered, wondering how Cindy had known to take the right-hand fork to Popocaxtil. Nothing about the road announced it as a likely candidate for anything but a dead-end logging track.

Ahead, lightning danced among the lowering clouds. Suddenly Trace wasn't so sanguine about rain washing Cindy into his arms. If she didn't know enough to pull over, park and wait out the storm, a good rain might wash her right off the mountain. The people who had made this road had neither known nor cared about grading the surface so that an out-of-control vehicle would slide into the mountainside rather than into the abyss. The road had been graded—if it had been graded at all—with rapid drainage in mind. Every slant led downhill. The farther up the road, the longer the downhill drop to the valley below.

As the afternoon wore on, Trace drove the Rover with near-reckless speed. The track became worse with every foot it climbed up the uninhabited mountainside. He paused only a few seconds at the spot where the Jeep had had its second flat. A single glance told him that there was only one set of footprints this time. Any tire changing that had been done had been done by the princess herself. One corner of his mouth curved up at the thought of how muddy she must have been by the time she had finished.

Then Trace wondered which one of Cindy's men had taught her to change a tire, and what else he had taught her to sweeten the lesson.

Trace pushed the thought away and concentrated on the road, which had dwindled until it required every bit of his skill and coordination, not to mention occasional applications of pure strength, just to keep the Rover pointed in the right direction. When the road pitched up suddenly, and simultaneously wrapped out and around a tight curve, he saw the broad marks left by Cindy's Jeep as it had slid sideways closer and closer to the lethal drop-off on the right side of the miserable road.

"Christ," Trace hissed between his teeth as he saw how close Cindy had come to disaster. "It's time someone put a leash on that high-nosed little . . ."

Trace's voice died as the Rover breasted the small ridge and he saw the burned-over valley spreading out below. A few hundred yards away, in the center of a deceptively smooth-looking stretch of road, a Jeep was buried up to its fenders in mud.

Smiling rather grimly, Trace let in the clutch and started toward the prey he had finally run to ground.

Three

——

Cindy didn't even notice the Rover cautiously working its way toward her. At that particular moment she wouldn't have noticed anything less impressive than a magnitude eight earthquake. She was bent over, panting and red faced, hopping around on one foot in the muck while she tried to force the broken-handled shovel into the muddy mess with her other foot. The point of the whole exercise was to ladle enough of the goo from the vicinity of the front tires so they could find the traction necessary to pull the Jeep out of the bog.

There was more gluey mud lying in wait than Cindy had the muscle or tools to remove. After more than an hour of shoveling she doubted that she was going to get the job done by herself. Unfortunately, there wasn't much hope of help. The surface of the road hadn't seen a wheeled vehicle since the last hard rain. If there were any native pedestrians about, they hadn't passed her way lately. Not so much as a

footprint marred the deceitfully smooth surface of the bog
ahead of the Jeep.

With a muttered word of disgust, Cindy watched the hole
she had just made with the shovel slowly fill up with goo.
She propped the slippery, much-too-short handle of the
shovel against the Jeep and decided there was no help for it,
she would have to go for more shrubbery. Wiping her hands
on equally muddy jeans, she released the cable on the winch
that was attached to the Jeep's front bumper. Rye hadn't
spent much time showing her how to work his Jeep's winch,
but she had remembered enough to get the thing unlocked
and started about an hour ago. Trial and error had re-
freshed her memory after that.

The first time Cindy had wrapped the cable around the
skeletal trunk of a burned tree, she had confidently expected
to winch the Jeep out of the mud. She had figured it would
take a lot of power, so she had given the winch everything
available. For a few moments the cable had whined taut and
the Jeep had indeed crept forward. Then the tree had ex-
ploded into charcoal and the cable had snapped back toward the Jeep with enough force to make the air whistle.

After that Cindy had gone back to shoveling until her
hands had stopped shaking. Then she had attempted to use
the winch again. All that had been within reach of the cable had been tree skeletons even more frail than the first one
she had tried to use. In the end she had settled for the vig-
orous green bushes and saplings that had grown up since the
fire. The first bush she used the winch on instantly leaped
out of the mud and bounded toward her. The second and
third bushes did the same. None of the shrubbery had held
long enough to move the Jeep forward so much as an inch.

The bushes had other uses, however. Cindy had discovered rather quickly that their branches could be beaten into
smaller pieces with the shovel and then pushed under the
Jeep's wheels to make a sort of rough mat that gave more
traction than straight goo did. That was how she had man-

aged to move forward a whole fourteen feet. At the present pace she would be out of the bog by nightfall...of next week.

Putting that unhappy thought from her mind, Cindy slogged over to the nearest shrub with the broken shovel in one hand and the cable hook in the other. Kneeling, using the shovel, she pushed the end of the cable around the base of the bush until she could grab the hook with her free hand, put it over the cable and stand up. As she turned to go back to the Jeep, she spotted movement on the road.

At first Cindy thought that the vehicle slipping and slithering half on and half off the road was a mirage coming toward her. When it came to a halt fifteen feet away—just before the point where her Jeep's wheels had sunk in to the fenders—she recognized Trace.

He was smiling.

Normally Cindy would have been the first one to laugh over the picture she must have made with mud up to her eyebrows and greenery sticking to unlikely parts of her anatomy. Unfortunately her reaction to Trace hadn't been normal from the first word they had exchanged. Suddenly Cindy was furious with Trace, with the Jeep, with the muddy road, with the world in general and Ecuador in particular; but most of all she was furious with herself for caring that she looked muddy and foolish in front of Mr. Trace Insufferable Rawlings.

When the Rover's door opened, Cindy turned her back on Trace and put the winch into motion with a vicious jerk. The bush fairly jumped out of the soil and raced toward her. She stopped the winch, lifted the shovel and began beating on the shrub until it had flattened out enough for her to release the hooked end of the cable without having to stand on her head in the muck to do so.

"Aren't you a little old for mud pies?"

The deep, amused male voice did nothing to cool Cindy's temper. She turned and slowly looked at Trace from the ground up. His lace-up jungle boots were scarred and clean where they rose above the mud. His khaki pants were clean, dry and tucked into the tops of his boots. Though loose fitting, the pants managed to convey very strongly the masculine power just beneath the cloth. His belt was wide, worn and fastened around a lean waist. An astonishingly big knife—more of a sword, really—was sheathed at his waist. His shirt was khaki, clean, dry, long sleeved, with cuffs rolled up just far enough to reveal tanned skin and a sheen of black hair stretched over sinewy arms. His hands were strong, long fingered and very clean. The black hair on his forearms was thickly repeated in a rich cloud that curled up from the open neck of his shirt. He had shaved since their last meeting. Somehow the clean, heavy line of his jaw was more intimidating than the careless masculine stubble had been.

Cindy looked no higher than the sensual lips curving beneath the black swath of Trace's mustache. The triumph and amusement in his smile made her own lips flatten. She told herself that she was a big girl, that she could take whatever teasing Trace dished out without losing her temper and making the situation worse by saying something.

And then she discovered that she was wrong. With a sense of mingled horror and pleasure she heard herself say, "I'm too old for a lot of things, Tarzan."

Cindy's black glance sweeping back down Trace's body hinted that he was foremost among those objects she had outgrown. Without another word she turned her back on him and resumed flattening the uprooted bush and stuffing it beneath the leading edge of her left front tire.

"You know, an intelligent girl like you should have figured out by now not to bite the hand that is going to feed her. But since you haven't, I'll be glad to deliver a little remedial instruction."

"You're too kind," she muttered, chopping viciously at the bush.

"I know. I also know if you'd been reasonable a few days ago instead of being a high-nosed princess who didn't know any more about men than to throw money at them, you could have spent the past two days doing your nails and have ended up no farther from Popocaxtil than you are now."

Cindy went very still. Slowly she released the shovel because she didn't trust herself not to take a swing at Trace with it. Part of her was appalled that she had even thought of it. Another part of her was appalled that she hadn't followed through. Three days ago she would have sworn that she knew herself through and through. Trace, unfortunately, brought out depths in her temperament that had remained blessedly hidden until she met him.

She knelt and began cramming brush around the tire by hand. Trace offered advice on the best type of greenery to use until she lost patience.

"Are you going to help get the Jeep out or are you just going to stand around and make noise?" Cindy asked without looking up.

"I'm waiting for a request. A nice one."

For an instant the world went an odd shade of reddish black in front of Cindy. Too many memories. Too many useless requests.

"Would you please," she said in a husky voice, *"go to hell?"*

Trace's green eyes narrowed as though he had been slapped. For a minute the only sound was that of soggy brush being rammed into the mud. Then came the distinct sucking sounds of Trace's boots as he walked back to his Rover. Cindy didn't look up. She simply continued blindly stuffing twigs and leaves and stems into the mud, furiously refusing to give in to tears or to memories, telling herself that she had come this far without Trace, she could go the rest of the distance alone, too.

The door to the Rover opened quietly and closed with emphasis. Trace sat back on the comfortable bench seat of the Rover and stretched his legs onto the passenger side of the floorboards. Confident of the outcome, he waited for Cindy to get tired of chewing on her pride, swallow hard, and ask him for the help she so clearly needed. Her learning when to ask for help—and how to ask for it—would make the rest of the trip a lot easier on both of them.

Trace had no intention of fighting Cindy every inch of the way while they 'searched' for her crazy friend. Not only would continual fighting be stupid, it could be dangerous. There were times and places in the wilds where questioning instructions was a fast way to get into deep trouble. If he said jump, she would have to learn to jump. If she needed help, she would damn well ask for it. That was the only way to ensure that she didn't put both of them in danger with her foolish stubbornness.

Combat pay. Well, you sure called it, Invers, you s.o.b.

A curse hissed between Trace's teeth. All fights between Cindy and himself would be won and lost right here, right now. She had chosen the battleground, the weapons, and the stakes—her pride. The only thing that remained for Trace to do was to accept her surrender so that they could get on with the farce of combing the wild country to find a woman who wasn't lost.

From Trace's vantage point in the Rover he could see the churned mess behind the Jeep. Twigs and slender branches with bruised and shredded leaves stuck up every which way on the sides of the deep ruts the Jeep had left. Idly, then with growing understanding, Trace's eyes followed the various trails Cindy had left through the mud as she had attached cables to bushes and dragged them to the Jeep.

The shattered remains of a charred tree raised Trace's dark eyebrows. *I hope that little fool didn't have the winch at high revs when that trunk came apart.*

Yet an uneasy prickling along Trace's spine every time he looked at the ruined tree told him that was precisely what had happened. Rather grimly he wondered if the crack in the

Jeep's windshield was old history or if the glass had given way from a recent hit delivered by a dangerous, whipsawing steel cable.

The longer Trace looked at the area immediately around the Jeep, the clearer it became to him that Cindy had been mired in place for a long time. Incredibly enough, and despite her demonstrable lack of expertise in such situations, she had managed to get the Jeep to move forward a few feet. Grudgingly Trace gave her credit for not sitting with her clean hands folded in her lap, waiting for a knight in muddy armor to rescue her.

Stubborn and resourceful, but that won't get the Jeep out of the muck. Even if it would, there's no way that soft rich girl is going to have enough strength to make mud pies much longer. Hell, it's a miracle she hasn't given up by now. She's got to be exhausted.

Fifteen minutes, Trace reassured himself silently, watching Cindy kneeling in the mud next to the front end of the Jeep. *Half an hour, max. Then she'll wise up and give up and do what she should have done in the first place—ask me for help.*

Trace was correct in his assessment of Cindy's reserves of strength. The past few days had exhausted her. Doing without food or drink so far today had been the final touch. She was running on adrenaline alone, supported by the rushing chemical wave of fury that came each time she looked up through the black, tangled curtain of her hair and saw Trace all dry and clean and comfortable, lounging in his Rover while he watched her crawl around in the muck.

Cindy winched another bush out and began beating on it with her shovel. When it came time to remove the cable from the mangled bush, her fingers were uncooperative. They insisted on trembling and tangling and slipping when they should have held firm. It was a good five minutes before she was able to retrieve and rewind the cable. Finally she picked up the shovel again and used its edge to smash and gnaw the bush into smaller pieces. One by one she shoved those pieces in the mud around the front tires.

Past experience had taught Cindy that she would need at least one more bush rammed into the muck before there would be enough traction for the Jeep. The prospect cheered Cindy considerably. Maybe this time she would get completely free of the bog and get on with looking for Susan. Even though the rational part of Cindy's mind kept insisting that Susan was an experienced traveler who had a positively feline ability to land on her feet no matter what the circumstances, the irrational part of Cindy's mind kept whispering about all the disasters that could befall a woman traveling alone in a foreign country.

For instance, Susan could have hired a guide like Trace Rawlings.

The surge of adrenaline that followed upon the heels of seeing Trace still ensconced within the dry, clean comfort of the Rover served to push Cindy through the mud, cable in one hand and shovel in the other. She was running out of conveniently placed bushes. On her hands and knees, and finally on her stomach, she maneuvered the cable until steel encircled the base of a bush. Slowly she slogged back to the Jeep, fired up the winch and reeled in the bush.

The bruised leaves of this particular bush smelled like the worst kind of swamp. Even more depressing, the five-foot-long branches were unusually springy, which meant that breaking each stick took twice the whacks with the shovel that an ordinary shrub would have. Finally, however, Cindy had the bush beaten and chopped into useable portions. Wearily she set aside the shovel, picked up a clump of vile-smelling greenery and began cramming it into the muck in front of one tire.

Trace looked at his watch for the thirtieth time in as many minutes. A half hour gone and Cindy didn't look much worse off than she had before. Obviously she was tired. Just as obviously, she wasn't going to give in. His lips flattened into a hard line beneath his dark brown mustache as he remembered what Invers had said: *Any woman who could stand up to Big Eddy could teach stubborn to a Missouri mule.*

Teeth clenched as tightly as her hands, Cindy trudged back toward the side of the road, dragging the winch cable in one hand and the shovel in the other. All that kept her from going down on her face in the mud and staying there when she hooked the cable around a bush was a bone-deep determination not to knuckle under to a man again, because once she did, she would lose more and more and more of herself until there was nothing left and she was just a shell standing and watching Jason walk away from her, taking her innocence, hopes and belief in herself with him.

But I learned from that, Cindy told herself firmly. *After Jason left I told Big Eddy to go directly to hell and to take his dreams of a dynasty with him. Then I changed my name, closed all the McCall expense accounts, and left home.*

Since then Cindy had not taken one dime from her father. She would speak to him as long as the subject of men, marriage or babies did not arise. If she didn't like what she heard—and she usually didn't—she would turn around and walk away. The kind of pride, intelligence and courage it had taken for Cindy to walk out on uncounted millions and make a life for herself was often labeled "character" when it occurred in men. When it cropped up in women, the labels applied were a good deal less flattering.

They were nothing, however, to the names Cindy called Trace as she fumbled around pushing more brush into the mud.

Trace looked from his watch to the muddy woman and mangled bush. His green eyes narrowed in a combination of irritation and grudging approval as the time registered.

Forty-seven minutes.

Absently Trace knuckled the hinge points of his jaw, trying to loosen muscles clenched in outright rebellion against sitting and doing nothing while a woman worked herself into the ground right in front of his disbelieving eyes.

She has to learn that I'm valuable to her or we're going to end up in big trouble in the cloud forest.

Somehow the lesson seemed less important to Trace at the moment than it had before.

Yet cold reason told him that the lesson was more important than ever. Cindy simply must give him a measure of control over their lives in the cloud forest. She had proven herself to be far too determined an individual for Trace to even consider fighting with her over every little aspect of the expedition.

If she would drive herself to exhaustion rather than admit that she needed his greater strength, to say nothing of his expertise, what would she do when an important issue arose, such as running for cover from a storm rather than continuing to drive on a road that would go from difficult to dangerous with the first good rain? What if he told her not to question some natives about Susan—and there were some natives in the backcountry who definitely should *not* be questioned—and she went ahead and asked questions anyway, endangering everyone with her stubborn certainty that she could do everything herself, and do it better?

Trace kept repeating that line of reasoning as he watched Cindy through hooded eyes, silently willing her to give in at least long enough to rest for a time.

She didn't. She simply kept after the task of freeing the Jeep with a tenacity he could only admire. Yet the more he watched, the less he could bear it. She was overmatched. He knew it even if she didn't. He found it too painful to see her working her heart out when he knew that eventually she would fail.

But Trace forced himself to watch the uneven contest between woman and bog. If Cindy could drive herself beyond all reason, the least he could do was to witness the brutal cost of her learning this particular lesson.

For both of them.

It would have been difficult to say whether Cindy or Trace was more relieved when she finally fumbled the last bit of brush into the mud and climbed into the Jeep.

At first it was enough for Cindy just to sit behind the wheel. Not to be bent over in the mud was sheer heaven. Besides, in the Jeep she was beyond the reach of the puddles. Their winking, reflective surfaces had been tormenting her with visions of drinking and drinking cool water until she was satiated.

"Not to mentioned drinking at the same time hundreds of miscellaneous and unpronounceable microscopic beasties that would make you so sick you'd be afraid you *wouldn't* die," Cindy reminded herself wearily. "No water for you until you're out of the bog and have time to boil up a quart or three."

Sighing, Cindy wiped her muddy hands on her muddy slacks and reached for the ignition key. Her hand trembled visibly. She closed her eyes and willed herself to be strong for just a bit longer. The Jeep would get free this time. It had to. She was too tired, too hungry and much too thirsty to do it all over again.

As always, the Jeep's engine fired up the first time. Cindy wiped her palms on opposite shoulder blades—the cleanest patches on her shirt—and gripped the wheel. Carefully she let in the clutch and fed gas. The front wheels slipped, spun, skipped, and finally bit into the mess of mud and shrubs. The Jeep lurched forward a few inches, slewed off to the right, found traction again, leaped and then swerved off to the left side of the road. The vehicle measured its own length in untouched muddy road, bucked, wallowed, whined...

And settled up to its fenders once more in the bog.

The sight of Cindy slumped over the steering wheel was too painful for Trace. After a single glance he looked away. Her posture stated her defeat more clearly than any words could have. He had won, she had lost...and the taste of victory was muddy on his tongue. He reached for the Rover's door, wanting to save Cindy the walk over to his vehicle to ask for help.

The Jeep's door popped open at the same instant as the Rover's. Cindy got out, sank calf-deep, and slogged to the front of the Jeep. It took her a long time to unlock the winch and drag the cable toward a big, particularly lush bush on the edge of the road. Though the bush was on the same side of the road as the Rover, Cindy didn't even glance toward Trace.

He closed his eyes, then opened them again. Nothing had changed. Cindy hadn't admitted defeat.

What is it with you, princess? Why is it impossible for you to give me a fraction of an inch? Would you ask me for help if my bank account was as big as yours?

Since the bitter questions never left Trace's mind, no answers came.

Cindy staggered, slipped and went down on her hands and knees. She stayed that way for a few moments, head down, beaten but unbowed. Slowly she pushed herself to her feet. Trace swore steadily, savagely, but he knew defeat when he stared it in the face. He could not force himself to sit and watch Cindy work until she fainted from exhaustion.

And that was what it would come to.

Nor would the bitter lesson have accomplished anything useful. Quite obviously the princess would drop dead in her muddy tracks before she lowered herself to ask for anything from a peon like Trace Rawlings.

So let her drop.

Trace didn't bother to answer his silent inner snarl. The sentiment was only the last defiant cry of the vanquished, and he knew it. There were some people he could have watched dispassionately while they drove themselves beyond exhaustion, but Cindy wasn't one of them. Bitterly cursing his weakness every step of the way, Trace closed the distance between himself and Cindy, who was almost up to the robust bush she had chosen to sacrifice beneath the Jeep's front wheels.

Just as Trace caught up to Cindy, she screamed chillingly and lashed out with the broken shovel at a snake that had been concealed within the bush.

Four

An instant later Trace slashed through the snake with his machete. Even as the big knife flashed past her, Cindy spun away from the bush in an effort to flee that was as reflexive as the trapped snake's strike at her had been. But Cindy went no more than a step before she discovered that her body was trembling too much for her to do more than sway on her feet. Trace held her upright with his left hand while he finished off the snake with the machete in his right hand. Only when he was quite certain that the reptile was dead did he sheathe the lethal blade, grab Cindy and carry her back to the Rover.

"Didn't anyone ever tell you that snakes don't make special allowances for stubborn princesses?" Trace demanded, his voice loud and rough with the adrenaline that was still pouring through his blood. Cindy had come within inches of dying, and while she was probably too naive to know it, he wasn't. "It's a damn good thing you got lucky with the shovel or that big 'two-step' would have nailed you on the first strike and you would have gone two steps and died. Do you understand me, princess? You would be d-e-a-d, *dead*. Where do you think you are—Disneyland? Didn't you even think to look for poisonous snakes?"

Cindy bit her lower lip and struggled to control the shudders racking her body in the wild aftermath of fear. "Rye always t-told me if I made p-plenty of noise, s-snakes would leave before I ever saw them."

"That doesn't mean you can close your eyes and braille your way through an Ecuadoran cloud forest," Trace snarled, wondering who the hell this Rye was. "Use your head! It's too cool, wet, and overcast for reptiles to be particularly lively right now, so the two-step felt trapped by you and it lashed out to protect itself. Thank God the snake was too sluggish to be any more than half-speed on the strike. You were lucky. Very, very damn lucky." Trace's arms tightened around the muddy, womanly weight in his arms. "But don't push it, princess. God has better things to do than to watch out for stubborn princesses."

"G-go to—"

"Hell," Trace interrupted impatiently, finishing Cindy's sentence for her. "You keep recommending the place to me. Perhaps you would like to join me there?"

He yanked open the passenger door of the Rover and slid in, still holding on to Cindy. When she struggled as though to get off his lap, Trace's arms tightened.

"Not a chance, princess. I came so close to putting you at the very top of my private list of midnight regrets that I'm not letting go of you for awhile. God, I can hardly believe you're alive," he said in a raw, husky voice as he smoothed his cheek over the tangled silk of Cindy's hair. "That was too close. Much too close." He felt the sudden shudders of her body and shifted her until he could cradle her in his arms. In a much more gentle voice he murmured, "It's all right. Go ahead and cry. You're safe now."

Cindy sensed as much as felt the caress of Trace's cheek over the crown of her head. She didn't cry despite the burning of her eyes and the ache of her throat. She had learned long ago that crying, like begging, was a waste of time and energy. What was going to happen would happen and neither her tears nor her pleas would make a bit of difference in the outcome.

She took in and let out a long, shaky breath and then another and another until she gradually relaxed across Trace's lap, her cheek on his left shoulder, her left hand tucked beneath his chin, her palm resting in the warm nest of hair that pushed up through his open collar. When he began to stroke her hair and spine with slow sweeps of his right hand, she sighed and shut her eyes, absorbing his comfort as if it were a balm.

Close up, the signs of Cindy's fatigue were all too obvious to Trace. Beneath random smears of dried mud, her skin was very pale, almost translucent. It was the same for her lips, nearly bloodless. Her eyelids showed dark lavender shadows of exhaustion. The slender lines of her hands were blurred by mud and the random cuts and scrapes that came from changing tires and winching bushes out of the ground. Her loose cotton clothes looked as though she had been packed in a mud bath and left to steam for an hour. Her blouse clung to her like a brown shadow. Her hands were smeared with mud, and so were her feet.

All in all, Trace had never seen a woman half so sexy to him . . . nor had he ever felt half such a heel.

The realization shocked him. It was utterly irrational. No sane man would prefer a muddy lap full of mulish stubbornness to the perfumed, practiced allure of the women he had known in the past, would he? No, of course not. No sane man would let himself in for the kind of grief a spoiled princess would inevitably deliver to her lover, would he? No, of course not. No sane man would . . .

Cindy sighed and snuggled fractionally closer to Trace's body, distracting him from his interior catechism on the subject of masculine sanity. Her breath stirred the hair below his throat and the distinctive, male flesh between his legs stirred in answer. He fought the nearly overwhelming impulse to pick up Cindy's hand and kiss her muddy little palm.

I've gone nuts.

Trace closed his eyes. It didn't help. It just made his other senses all the more acute. He felt the taut, full weight of Cindy's breasts resting against his chest, the rounded sweetness of her hips cradled between his thighs, the delicate touch of her breath and fingertips softly tangled in the hair just below his collarbone. He could also feel with razor clarity the heavy, deep beat of his own blood and the surging heat filling his loins, filling him.

Princess, what would you do if I peeled you out of those muddy jeans and unzipped my pants and fitted you over me like a hot velvet glove?

Trace's heartbeat doubled at the thought. His eyes snapped open. Very carefully he lifted Cindy from his lap and slid out the Rover's door, muttering something about getting her gear from the Jeep. Mud squelched and sucked at his boots all the way to the Jeep. He grabbed the two small suitcases from the back and tucked them under one arm. A folded tarp, mosquito netting and a sleeping bag went under the same arm. There was nothing left in the cargo area of the Jeep but the battered toolbox that had been bolted to the floor.

The front—and only—seat of the Jeep didn't offer much more in the way of supplies. Purse, empty canteen and a paper bag with a few discarded food wrappers were the only things Trace found. He grabbed the purse and canteen and went back to the Rover.

Cindy sat on the passenger side of the bench seat, watching Trace and wishing that he were in the car with her again.

She could still feel the imprint of his hard body and the gentle, reassuring sweeps of his hand over her. She hadn't felt so cherished since the months after her mother's death, when Rye would hear his little sister crying in the night and come to her room and lift her into his arms, rocking her until she fell asleep once more.

"Anything else?" Trace asked, looking into the clear, black eyes that watched him with surprising intensity. He felt an urge simply to stroke Cindy's tangled raven hair once more. The effort it took to control the impulse shocked him.

"Just the radiator water and gas cans," she answered.

Cindy's voice was somewhere between husky and raspy, as though her scream of fear had made her hoarse.

"They'll be okay for now," Trace said. "Do you feel strong enough to steer the Jeep while I winch it out of the muck?"

She blinked slowly, trying to focus on his words instead of on the sculpted line of his lips. "That's all? Just steering?"

Trace nodded.

Mentally Cindy took stock of herself. She had never been a tenth so tired. On the other hand, everything still worked, after a fashion.

"I can handle it," she said, as much to herself as to Trace.

Cindy started to climb out of the Rover, only to feel Trace's hard arms sliding beneath her knees and around her back once more. She made a startled sound as he lifted her from the Rover's bench seat and walked over to the Jeep as though she weighed no more than one of her soft-sided suitcases. He looked down at her surprised, mud-smudged, yet still elegant face. Beneath his dark mustache, one corner of his mouth kicked up slightly.

"I asked you about steering, not walking," he explained.

Trace saw the slow curving of Cindy's lips, felt the subtle changes in her body as she relaxed against him, and wanted

to laugh in triumph and howl with frustration at the same
time.

"A man of your word, is that it?"

As Trace looked down at Cindy again, all the laughter left
his face.

"Yes," he said simply.

For a long moment she stared into his intent green eyes.
At that moment he reminded her oddly of Rye, the only
man who had never failed her trust. Slowly she nodded.

"All right," Cindy said in a husky murmur. "I'll remember that."

Just as Trace reached the Jeep, Cindy spoke again.

"Trace?"

"Hmm?"

"Thank you."

"For this?" he asked, lifting her a bit higher.

"No. I mean, yes, but...the snake," she said simply.
"Thank you."

Trace's mouth flattened out and his arms tightened
around Cindy in unconscious protectiveness. "No need to
thank me. You got in the first shot."

"Luck. The snake was twice as long as that miserable
shovel handle."

Cindy watched as the powerful man holding her closed his
eyes, concealing their jungle green behind a dense thicket of
nearly black lashes. They were the only hint of softness in
Trace's suddenly bleak face.

"Don't thank me. I'm the fool who nearly got you
killed."

"That's ridiculous. You didn't put the Jeep in the bog or
the snake in the bush."

"I should never have allowed you to drive out of Quito,"
Trace said flatly.

"What do you mean, *allow*?" she retorted. "You had
nothing to do with it. I rented the Jeep the same way I drove
it—by myself!"

"And look where it got you."

Cindy looked up into Trace's narrowed green eyes and swallowed hard. "Into your arms?" she asked weakly.

Unwillingly Trace smiled even as he slowly shook his head. "Up to those sweet lips in mud, that's where," he muttered, outlining the curves of her mouth with a glance that revealed frank male hunger. "I can pull you out of the mud with no problem, but after that you might find yourself in bigger trouble than you were before."

Before Cindy could answer, Trace dropped her into the driver's seat of the Jeep and strode away. She watched with a mixture of envy and admiration as he maneuvered the Rover through the mud and into position with matter-of-fact strength and skill. The Rover had two winches, one in front and one in back. When the vehicles were roughly lined up Trace used the rear winch cable to attach the Jeep to the Rover.

The bigger, wider tires on Trace's vehicle spun through the fresh layer of storm-deposited silt to the older, more solid road beneath. The Jeep lurched forward, startling Cindy. She did her best to steer, but knew that it was the much heavier Rover and Trace's skill that were doing the real work. Together the two vehicles churned through the low stretch of the road and up the muddy incline on the opposite side.

The whole process took about three minutes.

Furiously Cindy's hands clenched around the wheel, wishing it were Trace's throat. He had barely gotten his boots dirty yanking the Jeep out of the bog, yet he had sat on his rump and watched her work her hands raw poking brush into the mud.

Waiting for her to ask him for help. *Nicely*.

It was just as well that Trace kept on driving rather than stopping to disconnect the two vehicles. Cindy was far too angry to pay much attention to details such as steering or clutch or accelerator. She was too furious to do anything but grit her teeth against the scream of pure rage that was trying to claw its way out of her throat. Her temper wasn't improved when a village appeared no more than ten minutes farther down the road.

"Damn him!" Cindy said with aching force. "*Damnhimdamnhimdamnhim!* If I had known, I could have walked here in half an hour!"

The object of Cindy's wrath divided his attention between the road ahead and the Jeep behind, towing Cindy to a spot just in front of the local cantina. As he parked, several old men looked up from their comfortable positions around a canted table. Cindy watched Trace walk over to the men before she got out and walked stiffly to the front of the Jeep. Without looking at Trace she began tugging at the cable, trying to release the Jeep.

"Leave it," called Trace. "We're not going anywhere today."

"Speak for yourself," Cindy muttered beneath her breath.

The next thing she knew her hands were being yanked away from the cable.

"I said leave it."

Cindy stared at Trace in mute, seething defiance.

"This is Popocaxtil," he said. "You wanted to come here, remember?"

She transferred her glare to his throat.

"Something bothering you?" Trace asked calmly.

"You. You're despicable. You knew you could get the Jeep out in a matter of minutes, but you let me work until I was cross-eyed."

Trace waited.

"And you knew all along that Popocaxtil was close by!"

It was more of an accusation than a question, but Trace answered anyway.

"Yes."

"But you didn't tell me!"

"You didn't ask." He looked at the high color that rage had brought to Cindy's mud-smudged cheekbones and inquired softly, "Anything you want to ask me now, princess?"

Trace waited, but Cindy simply turned away, dragged herself into the Jeep once more and sat with her head resting on the back of the seat and her eyes tightly closed.

"Suit yourself," he said, shrugging despite the anger simmering in his blood. "But then, princesses always do, don't they?"

With that Trace turned and went back to the men at the cantina. Cindy watched through slitted eyes while another rickety chair appeared out of nowhere. Trace sat down. From inside came a huge, thick-bodied woman carrying a heaped plate of food in one hand and a quart bottle of beer in the other. She set both in front of Trace.

Cindy's salivary glands ached in a sudden onslaught of hunger and thirst. She put them out of her mind. She would rather spit dust and starve to a skeleton than beg Trace for food or water. She would simply rest for a while. In half an hour or so she should have gathered enough strength to gesticulate with the natives until mutual understanding came. And with it, food and water.

"Water..."

She pulled herself into a fully upright position, blinked and looked around with real interest. As did most villages, Popocaxtil had a central well where its citizens drew water and gossiped.

Despite the exhaustion that made her clumsy, Cindy's determination hadn't diminished one bit. She leaned over the seat, fumbled in the toolbox until her hand finally connected with a tin pot from the mess kit, and pulled herself out of the Jeep. When she stood up she felt light-headed. She waited for the feeling to pass, then set off for the local well. No sooner had she filled the pot with cool, luscious water than Trace appeared like an evil jinni and dumped the water into the dirt.

"You little idiot! Have you been drinking the local water all along?" he asked harshly.

Cindy shook her head and looked wistfully at the spilled water. "I was going to boil it."

Trace let out a harsh breath. He took the pot in one hand and Cindy's grubby wrist in the other. "Did it ever occur to you that I might have water in the Rover?" he asked as he hustled her back to the vehicles. "Or did you figure that one peon's water is pretty much like another's, so you'd have to boil it all anyway?" Without waiting for an answer, Trace threw the pot into the back of the Rover and fished out his own canteen. He shoved it under Cindy's nose. "Drink."

She didn't wait for a second invitation. She fumbled the top off the canteen and began swallowing great mouthfuls of the wonderful water, not caring that some trickled from the corners of her lips. She had never tasted anything half so fine.

Eyes narrowed, Trace watched her. When she stopped for a breath he said, "How long have you been without water?"

Cindy looked at him over the canteen. "Not too—"

"How long?" he interrupted flatly.

"I ran out late yesterday," she said, her tone defiant. "I was going to boil some last night, but couldn't even find a puddle where I parked. Then I was so busy making mud pies today that I didn't get around to cooking any."

"And you would have died of thirst before asking for anything from a peon like me, right?"

"After I saw your smug smile when you pulled up and saw me in the mud, you're damned right!"

Trace remembered the paper bag with its few discarded food wrappers. "When was the last time you ate?"

"No problem. I can always live off the fat of the land," she said, smacking her right hip with her palm.

"How long since—"

"Yesterday," Cindy said, cutting across his words.

"And here I thought you were intelligent!" Trace's hands locked around Cindy's upper arms, hauling her up to within inches of his face. "Listen, princess. This is a wild land with mountains taller than God and meaner than hell. The cloud forest doesn't give one tinker's damn whether you're rich or poor, royalty or peon, dead or alive. And it's dead you're going to be if you don't climb down off your high horse. I'm not a bloody mind reader. If you want something—food or water or any other damn thing—*ask*. And when you're told to do something like leave the Rover's winch cable in place, *do it*. That particular winch has a tricky release. If you handle it wrong you'll lose a finger."

"If you had told me about the winch, I—"

"No," Trace said flatly, interrupting Cindy. He looked down into her defiant black eyes. "What happens when something goes wrong and there's no time for me to argue or explain? Should we both get injured or die because you're too spoiled and stuck-up to follow reasonable instructions? There can be only one leader of any expedition, and I'm the leader of this one. If you can't accept that I'll tie you in the Jeep and tow you all the way back to Quito."

Cindy wanted very much to tell Trace to roast his haunches in hell, but she knew that would be stupid—as stupid as some of the things she had already done. She didn't have the experience or reflexes to be on her own in the cloud forest, and she had proven it over and over. Going without food and water at a time when she needed every bit of her strength hadn't been one of her brighter moves.

But then, her IQ seemed to have been on hold since the first instant she had set eyes on Trace and felt dark fire licking beneath her skin.

"All right," Cindy said between her teeth. "You Tarzan, me Jane. Go for it."

"Are you asking me or telling me?"

She closed her eyes and wished she were twice as strong as Trace. Three times. Four.

"Ask me, princess."

But she wasn't strong. She was light-headed and tired and her tongue felt like a dirty mitten in her mouth.

"Have you ever," she said huskily, "had to beg for anything?"

"I'm not talking about begging, I'm—"

"Have you?" she demanded, cutting across Trace's words.

"No," he said curtly.

"I didn't think so." Cindy opened her eyes. They were as black and bleak as a night sky with neither moon nor stars. "I have. It won't happen again. Ever. So if you want the job of finding Susan Parker, I'll pay the way. If you want me to say 'pretty please, help me,' I'll find another way to follow Susan—because no matter how nicely I beg, you'll do what you damned well wanted to do all along, and you'll rub my nose in it every step of the way."

The bitterness seething beneath Cindy's matter-of-fact tone was almost tangible. Instinctively Trace's grip on her arms gentled until his palms were soothing over her in a slow caress.

"Is that what some man did to you?" Trace asked softly. "Make you beg and then humiliate you?"

There was a swift blaze of defiance, then nothing. Cindy's expression became as empty as her eyes. She had spent several years learning not to think about Jason's treachery. There was no reason to start remembering now.

"That has nothing to do with finding Susan," Cindy said.

For an instant Trace's grip hardened. Then he released her. "Susan was here over a week ago," he said, turning away. "She bought weavings and left for San Juan de Quextil."

Five

San Juan de...whatever," Cindy muttered, trying to remember the order of the villages from which Susan's cloth came. "That's not far."

Trace paused but didn't turn around. "It's on the next ridge over to the east."

"Good," Cindy said with relief. "We can be there before midnight."

"Not likely."

Cindy looked at the sky. The sun was already behind the flank of mountain but there was probably an hour of daylight left. As always, there were clouds of one kind or another hanging around, but no real rain threatened. "But the weather is fine."

"You aren't," Trace said bluntly. "You need food, a bath and sleep, in that order."

"But—"

"No."

Cindy clamped her mouth shut against her unspoken protests. *You Tarzan. Me Jane.* It was Trace's cloud forest and his rules. Arguing wouldn't change anything.

Besides, she was too tired to argue.

Without looking back to see how his curt refusal had settled with Cindy, Trace walked into the cantina. Once inside he fought a sharp struggle with himself. He lost. Cursing his lack of willpower when it came to one Cindy Ryan, he tracked down the monumental waitress. He had promised himself that he would make Cindy ask for whatever she needed, but the thought of her being thirsty or hungry defeated him. He would get the expedition on some kind of normal footing once she was fed and rested. Until then he wouldn't be able to look at her dirty, wan face without wanting to turn himself in to the nearest police station and start confessing to crimes he'd never even heard of, much less committed.

Ten minutes later, when Trace emerged from the cantina carrying food, Cindy was curled awkwardly in the front seat of the Jeep, sound asleep.

I'll bet if I'd said she needed sleep, food and a bath, in that order, I'd have found her skinny-dipping in the village well, Trace thought in exasperation, looking down at the tangled cloud of black hair fanned across the seat. *Maybe if I tell her to sleep in the Jeep tonight she won't argue about the two of us sleeping in the only bed in the only room in town.*

Trace reached into the Jeep and shook Cindy awake. The instant she began to mumble protests at being dragged into consciousness he shoved a plate of food under her nose. The effect was immediate and salutary. Black eyes opened, focused on the mounds of tiny potatoes and roast chicken and corn tortillas. Cindy inhaled the fragrance and reached for the food. The sight of her dirty fingers stopped her in mid-reach.

"Your shower won't be ready for a few minutes," Trace said in a clipped voice. An impatient snap of his wrist unrolled the damp makeshift hand towel he was carrying. He dumped it over her wrists. "I'll be back for the plate. It had better be clean."

With that Trace went to the Rover and began unloading it. Cindy was too busy wiping her face and hands to notice what Trace was doing. Halfway through her cleanup, when the soft white cloth she was using had become irretrievably dirty, she looked closely at it and made a startled sound. She was industriously grinding mud into a formerly clean T-shirt. From its size, it could belong only to one man—Trace Rawlings.

"Well, it's too late now," Cindy muttered. "I might as well make a thorough job of ruining it."

She finished wiping her fingers and face clean before she attacked the plate of food with outright greed. The flavor of the roast potatoes was unexpected, delicate and utterly delicious. The chicken had a chocolate sauce that was equally unexpected and not so delicious. The meat was as tough as the tortillas were savory and tender. She ate everything without a pause, deciding that the odd chocolate sauce improved upon longer acquaintance.

When Trace came back half an hour later, Cindy's eyes were closed and her plate was empty of all but a pile of neatly gnawed bones. He hoped having a full stomach would improve her mood. He reached down to awaken her, then stopped, staring at the luminous, fine-grained skin framed by wings of raven hair. She was breathing deeply, easily, and the tiniest crumb of tortilla was tucked into a corner of her full lips.

Slowly Trace withdrew his hand. If he touched Cindy, he would bend down and lick up the small crumb . . . and then he would slide his tongue into Cindy's warm mouth and kiss her the way he had wanted to since he had first seen her in the smoky Quito bar.

"Your bath is ready," Trace said, his voice deep.

Cindy stirred. Trace watched hungrily while her rosy tongue roved over soft, very pink lips, tasting the recent food and licking up the tiny crumb. She started to sit upright, groaned softly, and curled into another uncomfortable position in the bucket seat.

"Can you walk or do you want me to carry you?" Trace asked finally, hoping Cindy would opt for walking. If he felt her weight in his arms right now he wouldn't be responsible for the kiss he would surely demand of those deep pink lips.

"Mmph."

"Mmph," Trace agreed, sighing, not knowing whether to smile or swear at the opportunity that had just presented itself.

He plucked Cindy from the Jeep's front seat, carried her through a side door of the cantina and into a tiny room. There were wooden slats on the floor, a rusty pipe poking out of the wall and a bar of improbably blue soap stuck to a high window ledge. Her own shampoo, conditioner and comb had been set out near the door, along with a towel bearing the initials TER.

"You awake?" Trace asked softly.

She murmured a sleepy negative.

"Good."

Slowly Trace let Cindy slide down his body and onto her own feet. He didn't let go of her, simply shifted his arms until she fit his body the way mist fit the mountainside, seamlessly, no gaps and nothing in between. He stared down at her lips and wondered if she tasted half as sweet as she looked. With a final, silent curse at his lack of self-control where this one woman was concerned, he bent and fitted his mouth over hers with exquisite care, leaving no sensitive surfaces untouched.

For a few moments Trace moved his head slowly, parting Cindy's lips by fractions, feeling the subtle changes in her body tension as she went from dazed sleep to sensuous half wakefulness. Suddenly he could wait no longer to taste her. He twisted his head hungrily.

Cindy's mouth opened in surprise and response to Trace's kiss, leaving her vulnerable to the velvet penetration of his tongue. She could neither speak nor move, so tightly was she held in Trace's arms. She had no physical defenses against the slow, hot glide of his tongue. Nor did she have any mental defenses against the consuming kiss, for she had never been kissed with a tenth so much heat, even by the man she had once thought to marry.

With a throttled moan Cindy gave herself to Trace's embrace, moving her tongue over his, tasting him more and more deeply with each racing second until they were locked together in a searching kiss that turned her bones to honey.

The abrupt appearance of the floor beneath Cindy's feet came as a distinct surprise to her. So did the sudden feeling of emptiness when Trace's mouth lifted from hers. Slowly she opened her eyes, aware of a distinct feeling that she had just made a mistake. A bad one. She hadn't been the least bit aroused by any man since Jason, her first lover. And— she had vowed—her last. If she were going to make an exception to that particular personal rule, she knew she should have started with someone a good deal less potent than Trace Rawlings. He was way beyond her level of sensual experience.

But he tempted her almost unbearably. The late golden sunlight slanting into the washroom through the high window made his eyes luminous, nearly emerald in color, twin green fires watching her.

"I do believe I've finally found a way to communicate with a high-nosed little princess," Trace said, smiling, bending down to Cindy's mouth again.

Cindy stiffened and tried to ease from Trace's arms. She didn't have the least bit of success. He was even stronger than he looked, holding her effortlessly, hotly. The caress of his mustache on her sensitive, flushed lips made goose bumps march up and down her arms.

"Now don't get your ruff up," Trace murmured, nibbling along Cindy's lower lip. "All I meant was that since you have such a hard time with words, it only made sense for me to give you another way to thank me for waiting on you hand and foot."

"Generous of you," Cindy managed through clenched teeth.

"I thought so. Care to build up your account against future maid service?" he asked, running the tip of his tongue along her closed lips.

"No thanks," Cindy said coolly, feeling like a fool for having responded so completely to Trace when the kiss had been nothing more than a casual joke to him. "I always take care of maid service with a generous tip."

Trace straightened and released her. "Wide awake now, aren't you, princess?"

"Better late than never."

"Not as far as I'm concerned. The sleepy version is a hell of a lot more woman."

"Woman isn't a synonym for stupid," Cindy retorted.

"I know. I'm surprised you do, though."

With that Trace walked out and closed the door behind him. His voice came back through the badly fitted slats, warning Cindy that she had only fifteen minutes to get clean. She shut her eyes, got a grip on her fluttering nervous system, and turned on the shower.

A thin, erratic stream of cool water came out of the pipe. She looked at her clothes, shrugged, and stepped under the water. Working quickly she wet down and lathered everything from crown to heels with her shampoo, rinsed, and then peeled down to underwear and repeated the process. By the time her hair had been conditioned and rinsed once more, she was feeling deliciously clean.

She turned off the water, which was down to a trickle by now, shed her clothes, wrung them out and her hair as well, and examined her soggy tennis shoes with a rueful smile. They had been white to begin with. Now they were a kind of ruined beige. It was the same for her blouse and slacks. Though clean, they were randomly stained by brown mud and traces of green vegetation.

"Oh, well," Cindy muttered to herself. "Some women pay a fortune for just that kind of tacky tie-dyed look."

She picked up the towel, dried herself quickly, then rolled her clothes up in the big towel, squeezed hard, and squeezed some more.

Trace knocked on the door and called, "Time's up."

"Wait!" Cindy called, unrolling her bikini underpants and pulling them on frantically. "I'm not dressed!"

"Is that an invitation?"

"Don't you dare!" she said, cringing against the clammy cups of the bra as she fastened it in place with flying fingers.

"A dare is better than an invitation any day," he drawled.

"Dammit, Trace . . . !"

Cindy knew that pulling the damp slacks quickly over her curvy hips was out of the question. She jammed her arms through the short sleeves of her blouse and pulled the clammy sides together over her full breasts.

"Relax," Trace said, opening the door and walking in, unbuttoning his shirt with one hand, carrying clean clothes with the other. "You've got nothing I haven't seen before, and vice versa."

After Trace hung the clothes on a nail and shut the door, he was no more than a foot away from Cindy in the tiny room. For several frozen instants she stood with damp slacks dangling from one hand and towel from the other as she stared at the bare male chest emerging from the shirt. Technically what Trace had said was perfectly correct. She had seen shirtless men before, and had seen Jason wearing nothing more than a triumphant smile.

But seeing Trace was a whole different order of experience. Jason had been good-looking, but not...compelling. Trace exuded a kind of potent, effortless masculinity that went beyond the swirling patterns of dark brown hair and the supple bands of muscle crossing his chest. He was intensely vital, overflowing with heat and life, and he had set her on fire with a single deep kiss, something that Jason hadn't managed to do with the sum total of all his lovemaking.

Cindy didn't realize that she was staring at Trace until his hands went to his waist. Her breath caught with a small sound that was lost beneath the hiss of his descending zipper. She spun and faced the wall. He laughed.

"You are de..." Cindy said angrily, but couldn't force any more syllables past the breath wedged in her throat.

"Desirable?" Trace taunted.

She made a choked sound. He laughed deeply, enjoying himself for the first time since Quito, when he had sensed the dark fire burning within Cindy. Well, he was enjoying himself for the second time, to be precise. He had enjoyed kissing her far too much for his own comfort. Teasing her was a lot safer, as long as he kept his pants mostly on. "And here I thought spoiled, overcivilized women liked being turned on by peons."

"Says who?"

"D. H. Lawrence," Trace said smoothly.

Cindy's mouth snapped shut. By an immense effort of will she managed to ignore Trace long enough to wriggle into her wet slacks.

"Our room is the second door to the left. And don't wander too far in those clothes, princess. They don't conceal nearly as much wet as they did dry."

The door closed behind Cindy with a distinct thump. She looked down at herself, made a stifled sound, and fled to the privacy of the second door on the left. Not until she was inside with the door safely shut did the implication of Trace's words sink in.

"*Our* room?" she asked in a raw voice, looking around.

There wasn't much to look at. The sagging bed was either a generous single or a stingy double mattress lying flat on the floor. There was a blanket but neither sheets nor a pillow. Rugs, curtains, electricity and running water were also among the missing amenities. Not to mention privacy. She couldn't even lock the door for the simple reason that there was no lock in sight, not even a dead bolt or a chair to wedge under the door handle.

And Trace's duffel bag was sitting with her suitcases on the floor, right next to the lone mattress.

Cindy peeled off her wet clothes and pulled on dry ones, moving quickly, not knowing how long she would have before Trace finished his shower. She did know that she wasn't going to be caught in see-through clothing again. Not that it had bothered Trace. For all the response he had shown, she could have been wearing the ratty blanket that was folded haphazardly at the foot of the even rattier mattress.

For his part, Trace spent an unusual amount of time in the shower, trying to forget the picture Cindy had made when he had walked into the washroom. The deep, rich curves of her body had been a shock to him. She must have worked very hard choosing clothes that would minimize the sweet contrast of her small waist with her taut, full breasts and hips. Graceful feet, long legs, a lush triangular shadow balanced at the apex of her thighs . . . and nipples gathered into deep, pink pouts by the wet cloth of her blouse.

Trace had wanted her just that way, cold cloth and hot flesh and his tongue shaping her nipples into hungry velvet daggers. Just the thought of it brought a grating sound from deep in his throat. He had seen other women wearing much less, but not one of them had brought his body to immediate, full alert. Cindy had. He was still hard, throbbing, so hot he half expected to hear the water sizzle on his skin.

One bed. God. She's so damned soft and that floor is going to be so damned hard. Maybe she'll take pity on me and let me sleep next to her.

Yeah, sure. And maybe all her money will turn to grass and the cow that jumped over the moon will eat it and give green milk.

By the time Trace had finished his shower and dressed in clean clothes, his body had reluctantly accepted the message his mind was sending: *Forget it.*

For Trace to be stuck on an expedition with a spoiled princess who had taken one look down her nose at him and decided he could be bought out of her petty cash account was bad enough. To let her get the upper hand because he wanted her would be the dumbest thing he had ever done in a long life studded with dumb things.

For God's sake, she can't even lower herself to ask me the time of day, and here I am tying myself in knots wanting her?

I'm nuts. That's all there is to it.

Nuts!

Angry with himself, the world, and the thought of a long night on a hard floor, Trace stalked down the unlighted hallway to the bedroom. After a perfunctory knock he walked in.

Cindy had changed from her wet clothes into a pair of slacks that were loose everywhere a pair of pants could be loose—waist, hips and legs. The blouse was big enough to double as a pup tent. Trace knew he should have been grateful that Cindy was no longer wearing sexy, water-slicked, transparent cotton, but he wasn't. It was irritatingly obvious that she was making a special effort to be as unappealing to him as she could manage to be.

"You mug the waitress for that outfit?" Trace asked, balling up and tossing aside his dirty clothes.

Cindy looked down at her slacks and shirt. Handwoven from hand-dyed natural fibers, the clothes were colorful, unstructured and very fashionable, as well as sinfully comfortable.

"This is one of Susan's designs."

"No wonder she's lost. She can't follow the lines of a woman's body, much less a road map."

"She made it to Popocaxtil," Cindy shot back.

Trace grunted and looked around. "That's no recommendation."

Cindy took a better grip on her temper. No one had ever been able to pull her cork quite so quickly, not even Rye at his most maddening.

Trace glared at her. "You know, for someone who's so blazing fond of Susan Parker, you sure aren't very curious. You haven't even asked me if the villagers knew anything else about her but the fact that she left."

"You know I care about Susan. If you learned anything else—and if you want to tell me what that is—you will. My asking won't make a bit of difference."

Despite the cool neutrality of Cindy's words, she watched Trace with anxious eyes.

"The villagers sold her some cloth, food and gasoline and went about their own business. They said she was *muy hermosa*, very beautiful," Trace added almost grudgingly, "and that she spoke with her hands and her smile."

Cindy let out a long breath and relaxed, reassured about Susan for the first time since her friend had turned up missing.

"That's Susan," she said eagerly, her eyes alive with laughter. "Cinnamon hair and the kind of slender, willowy body that looks good in everything, and she can make anyone understand anything with that stunning smile of hers and a wave of her elegant hands. If she had turned up covered with mud the way I was, she'd have started a new fashion rage."

"Is this where I'm supposed to gallantly point out that you're hardly a dog yourself?"

The cool sarcasm in Trace's voice took the laughter right out of Cindy's eyes.

"Gallant? You?" she retorted incredulously, thinking of how Trace had sat and watched her struggle to free the Jeep. "Not very damn likely. For instance, the *gallant* thing to do with one mattress, one man and one woman is for the man to—"

"Put a cork in it, princess," Trace said coldly, slicing across Cindy's words. "I'll sleep on the floor tonight but not out of any misplaced sense of gallantry. Sharing a lumpy mattress just isn't worth putting up with your grief."

Ignoring Cindy, Trace began making the mattress into a bed. First he removed the musty wool blanket and dumped it into a bare corner of the room. With an expert flip of his wrist he spread his tarp over the mattress. When he began untying Cindy's sleeping bag she made an involuntary noise. She was too violently aware of Trace as a man to be comfortable sleeping in the same room with him, no matter who was on the mattress and who was on the floor.

Trace looked up suddenly, pinning Cindy with his icy green glance. "Relax. I'm not going to stick my hand up your blouse while you're asleep. I won't crawl into bed with you, either. And crawling is what you'd make a man do to get close to you, isn't it, princess? Well, I just don't crawl worth a damn. The sooner you figure that out, the easier this trip will be on both of us."

With another impatient movement of his wrist, Trace unrolled Cindy's sleeping bag so quickly that the cloth made a snapping noise as it settled over the mattress. She waited until he let go of the bag before she bent over and retrieved it. Saying nothing, she turned and went to the door, grabbing her own tarp along the way. She barely had the door open when Trace's hand shot over her shoulder and slammed the door shut in front of her face.

"Planning on sleeping in the hall?" he asked in a deceptively soft voice.

Cindy wasn't going to answer, but a single glance over her shoulder at Trace's face told her that he would get his answer one way or another. "No. In the Jeep."

"You'll be more comfortable lying in the bed than sitting up in the Jeep."

"I'm used to it. Besides, after a day of making mud pies, I'm tired enough to sleep standing up. As your day has been considerably less strenuous," she added with a cool smile, "I'm sure you'll appreciate the mattress more than I would. And don't worry, Mr. Rawlings. Where I sleep won't have the least effect on your tip."

Trace hissed a searing word under his breath and turned his back on Cindy. He didn't move until he heard the door open and close behind him. Then he stripped off his clothes, turned off the battery-powered lantern he had brought from the Rover and lay on the contested mattress.

He was still awake when it began to rain.

Six

The luminous dial of Trace's watch told him that he had been lying on the lumpy mattress for nearly an hour. He had counted sheep, goats, llamas, alpacas, mice and raindrops, all to no avail. He was no closer to sleep than he had been when he went to bed. Even worse, he had run out of new ways to curse himself as a fool and the old ways had lost their zing.

"Hell."

In a single motion Trace shot off the low mattress and stood glaring toward the inoffensive bedroom door. It was quite obvious that Little Ms. Rich Britches wasn't adult enough to admit her mistake and come in out of the rain. That meant that he would have to be adult enough to point her mistake out to her and drag her back inside.

Muttering to himself, Trace yanked on the clean underwear and slacks he had laid out by the mattress. He groped around in the dark until he found the tiny pencil flashlight he had put at the head of the mattress. With a tiny clicking sound the light came on. He found and scuffed into his boots before he stalked out the door, making less noise than the softly falling rain.

Though it was hardly late at night by city standards, the cantina building and the village were absolutely dark. Out in the countryside a rooster was the only clock that kept local time. Trace knew the territory, so he never traveled without a variety of battery-powered lights, one of which was the flashlight that was no bigger than his index finger. The penlight generated a very narrow, very sharp shaft of illumination. Rain fell in gentle silver veils through the cone of light. With another exasperated curse Trace stepped into the rain and stalked to the nearby Jeep. The moldy canvas top was up, but he knew that it must leak somewhere. Canvas always did.

As soon as Trace opened the door he knew where the Jeep leaked. Everywhere. Water ran in cool trickles across the ceiling and down the sides of the canvas top, with occasional diversions down his neck as he stared in disbelief at Cindy. She had the tin mess-kit pot underneath the biggest area of drips, which happened to be left of center in the driver's seat. The other leaks were deflected from the passenger side by a ground tarp Cindy had pulled up to her neck. Beneath the tarp was her sleeping bag, which she had opened and used as blanket. Despite having curled herself almost double, her bare feet stuck out from under the tarp. A trickle of water splashed onto her toes every so often. Water dripped into the tin pan with monotonous regularity.

Cindy was asleep.

Trace stared at her, not knowing whether to swear or to take his stubborn princess into his arms. It was a conflict he was becoming accustomed to the longer he was around her.

In the end Trace gave in, a bittersweet solution to which he was also becoming accustomed. There was really no other choice this time, as there had been none the other times. I

Cindy stayed in the Jeep, by morning she would be stiff, sore and doubtless sick into the bargain. And Trace had little doubt that Cindy was more than exhausted enough to sleep despite all the running water. After all, he was the gallant knight who had sat and watched her work until she staggered, all in the name of teaching her how to ask for help when she needed it.

Obviously the lesson hadn't been learned.

"Princess," Trace muttered in a low, gritty voice, "what the hell am I going to do with you?"

There was no answer but the hollow sound of water drops running onto the tarp and from there onto Cindy's soft flesh. Swearing, Trace tucked the penlight behind his ear as a makeshift miner's light. Gently he removed the wet tarp and extricated Cindy from her uncomfortable, leaky bed.

"At least you could have slept in the Rover," Trace continued in a husky, reasonable voice. He arranged Cindy in his arms and tucked in trailing edges of her sleeping bag so that he wouldn't trip. "It doesn't leak and you would fit nicely on the front bench seat. But no, you wouldn't even ask for that much from a peon, would you?"

He sighed a sibilant curse. "One of us is going to have to smarten up a bit, princess, or you're going to keep on being too proud to take a peon's advice and then you'll end up hurting yourself before I can stop you. Then I'll feel lower than a snake's belly and I'll take it out on you and you'll get your ruff up and try to walk on water or something equally stupid and then we'll be back where we were a few minutes ago—me lying awake and you fishing for pneumonia in a leaky Jeep."

Cindy's only answer was a murmured word that Trace didn't catch. Protecting her from the rain as best he could, he carried her to the cantina, then ducked in through the side door and down the dark hallway leading to the small room. He went in and shut the door behind him with his foot, then knelt and put Cindy on the mattress. She stirred

again. Her fingers clung to him when he would have withdrawn.

"Rye?" she murmured.

Trace froze in the act of turning off the penlight.

"Rye?" she repeated, her voice growing stronger.

"Yes," Trace lied softly through his gritted teeth. "It's
Rye." He turned off the light and tucked it alongside the
mattress. "Go to sleep, love. I'm here. Everything is all
right."

Cindy murmured something contented that Trace
couldn't understand. Her hands linked sleepily behind his
head and her cheek sought the warmth of his naked chest
once more. He fought a short battle with his conscience,
won, and lay down beside her. He pulled her lightweight
sleeping bag over both of them.

With a sigh Cindy curled trustingly against Trace's body
and sank into a deep sleep again. His hands clenched into
fists as he felt the sweet weight of her breasts against his
chest and wondered who the hell Rye was. Who was the
paragon of humanity Cindy trusted enough to give herself
into his keeping without struggle or hesitation? And why in
God's name wasn't dear, no doubt *gallant* Rye in Ecuador
with Cindy right now, keeping her out of Trace's hair and—
more to the point—out of his arms?

Trace breathed in deeply, feeling the warm, spicy fragrance of Cindy radiate throughout his body. What sane
man would let a woman like this go off into the wilds alone?

"You're crazy," Trace whispered aloud, his voice a soft
rasp.

He had all night to think just who was crazy—Rye, Cindy,
or Trace Rawlings.

The woman in Trace's arms breathed softly, her breasts
stirring subtly against his chest with each breath, her
warmth tangling with his own. Their bodies were equally
tangled. His left arm encircled her narrow waist; her torso

lay half on his. Her right arm was stretched across his chest and her fingers were tucked into the warm nest of hair beneath his left arm. Her leg lay between his, her thigh so close to his rigid male flesh that he was afraid to breathe. If she accidentally touched him . . .

And it would be even worse if she didn't.

Trace couldn't stifle the groan that leaked between his clenched teeth. The hunger for Cindy that had nearly brought him to his knees in the shower yesterday had tormented him all night. He had slept little and had awakened so aroused that he ached from his neck to his knees. He had spent all the long hours of darkness that way. The night hadn't been a total loss, however. He had definitely decided who was crazy.

He was.

Very carefully Trace eased away from the smooth, fragrant woman who had shared the mattress with him in a night of unaccustomed chastity. At least it had been unaccustomed for Trace. He had never spent the night with a woman he wanted and not taken her. Nor had he ever spent the night with a woman he hadn't wanted. At the moment he was too aroused to decide if that made two more rules he had broken for Cindy, or only one.

Why not just smooth her legs apart and wake her up from the inside out? If that kiss in the washroom was any sample, she wouldn't mind a bit.

That is the dumbest idea you've had in months! Trace told himself savagely as he rolled off the mattress and stood up.

Wrong. The dumbest idea was doing Invers a favor by getting Big Eddy McCall off his back.

Trace sighed and rubbed his face with his palms, wishing he could get his hands on Invers. But that was impossible. The only thing within reach was a stubborn princess whose eyes and body burned with dark fires she wouldn't let him touch. Cursing Invers and Big Eddy and everything but the softly sleeping woman who was too close and much too far away, Trace rubbed his face harder. Beard stubble rasped back. Without stopping to question why he was bothering to shave when he wasn't even in the lowlands, Trace picked up his shaving kit and silently left the room.

Cindy awakened moments later. Eyes closed, she stretched luxuriously. Suddenly she made a startled noise and sat up, looking around wildly in the semidarkness. She remembered falling asleep in the Jeep and nothing else. Obviously this wasn't the Jeep.

"Trace?"

There was no answer. Slowly Cindy inventoried her surroundings once more. The room was familiar enough. Her suitcases were still there. So was Trace's duffel bag. Ditto for his battery lantern and sandals and a pencil flashlight tucked alongside the mattress. She was covered with her own sleeping bag, which she had opened up to make into blanket last night in the Jeep. She was resting on top of Trace's sleeping bag, which had been similarly unzipped. There was no other bed in sight, not even a makeshift pallet on which Trace could have slept.

The only possible conclusion was that Cindy had spent the night, or at least part of it, sleeping with Trace Rawlings.

Relax, princess. I'm not going to stick my hand up your blouse while you're asleep.

Too sleepy to marshal her usual defenses, Cindy admitted to herself that there was nothing she would have liked better than to awaken with Trace's hand caressing her breasts. Even the thought made her shiver, tightening her nipples until they stood out against the loose cloth of her blouse. The bittersweet irony of her situation made her want to laugh and cry at the same time. She had given up hope of finding a man who would want her instead of her money. She had given up men, period. Then along came Trace Rawlings, a man she found she wanted very much...a man who had kissed her once and apparently had decided that kissing her was more trouble than it was worth.

Crawling is what you'd make a man do to get close to you, isn't it? Well, I don't crawl worth a damn.

A slow, hot flush crawled up Cindy's body as she remembered Trace's icy words. Was that how she seemed to him—a woman whose greatest pleasure was in humiliating men, making them beg for a kiss or a smile?

Teeth scored Cindy's lower lip as she shook her head in silent denial of Trace's indictment. She had once been humiliated in just that manner by a man. She would never make another human being submit to that kind of cruelty any more than she would force herself to crawl for any man again, no matter what the reason. Maybe if she explained that to Trace they could start all over again.

Maybe this time he would want her instead of being angry with her.

"Oh, sure," Cindy muttered, rolling out of bed and standing up. "He's the very soul of understanding and gallant forgiveness. You knew that the instant you looked up from the mud and saw a smug smile plastered on his handsome face."

Gloomily Cindy began packing everything. She had to roll the sleeping bags several times each before she was satisfied that they wouldn't come undone the instant someone picked them up, which was what her own sleeping bag had done the first time she had rolled it. The dirty clothes she had collected without regard for ownership went into the big plastic garbage bag she had packed for just that purpose. Her tennies were still soggy and none too appealing, but a pair of dry socks made it possible to squeeze her feet into the shoes.

With a feeling of foreboding, Cindy pulled her small travel mirror out of her suitcase. A single glance told her more than she wanted to know.

"No wonder Trace couldn't wait to get out of bed this morning," she said, grimacing. "I've seen better looking women riding brooms on Halloween."

A small brush and a lot of patience took the snarls from Cindy's hair. She looked at her makeup kit, shrugged, and put on a minimal amount, not wanting to call attention to herself by wearing something as useless as blusher in a cloud forest. The result of her sketchy pass with the makeup kit was depressingly less than spectacular. And, to be honest, she wouldn't have minded looking spectacular for Trace, if only to prove to him that she could be a desirable woman.

"Hey, princess. You awake?"

At the sound of Trace's voice Cindy guiltily buried her mirror in the dirty clothes bag.

"Yes."

"Good. Get the door, will you?"

Cindy opened the door and tried not to stare. Trace was wearing an old black T-shirt whose soft knit fitted perfectly over his chest, underlining every powerful shift of muscle and tendon. His slacks were khaki, loose, yet they managed to remind her with every movement he made that there were long, muscular legs just beneath the cloth. His dark hair was glistening from the shower, showing a hint of curl in its thick depths. Clean shaven but for a mustache, his face revealed its uncompromising Scandinavian planes. Beneath very dark, steeply arched brows, his eyes were gemlike in the clarity and intensity of their green color.

Cindy had never seen a man who appealed to her senses more. It was all she could do not to reach up and trace the clean masculine lines of Trace's eyebrows, his lips, his jaw, and then to kiss him as she finally had in the shower. Only this time she wouldn't freeze up. She wouldn't stop kissing Trace until he was trembling as much as she had yesterday. If such a thing were possible.

A thoughtful frown settled onto Cindy's face as she wondered if men ever got so aroused that they trembled. If

she asked Trace about it, would he answer her or simply
make fun of her obvious lack of experience?

"Hello?" Trace said, wondering why Cindy was staring
at him as though he were an utter stranger. "Remember me?
Your intrepid guide?"

Cindy stepped back hastily from the doorway, feeling a
blush heat her cheeks. "Er, yes, Come in."

"Here," said Trace, holding out a plate on which was
balanced a cup of coffee, a mound of eggs and a wad of
tortillas. "This will take the cobwebs out of your brain."

Wordlessly Cindy accepted the plate, staring at Trace as
though he were a magician. She had been so busy drinking
in his appearance that she hadn't even realized he was holding two plates in his hands. And very intriguing hands they
were—tanned, long fingered, lean, strong, the backs pat-
terned with the same glossy dark brown hair that curled up
from the vee neck of his shirt.

"Coffee," Trace explained, giving Cindy a sideways
glance when she made no move to eat or drink.

She didn't notice the glance. She was looking up the bare
length of his forearms, tracing the exquisitely masculine
textures of tanned skin and very dark, shiny hair, and the
flex and flow of muscle with each motion of Trace's body.
She wanted to run her fingertips and cheek and lips over his
arm, outlining each warm ridge of muscle and tendon.
Would he like that? Would it shorten his breath just a little? Would it make him look at her as though she were a
desirable woman rather than a useless albatross tied around
his neck?

"Are you all right?" Trace asked finally, glancing at
Cindy's hands, which were clenched so tightly on the plate
that her knuckles were pale.

"No." Cindy closed her eyes and wondered at the turmoil of her mind and the curious, slow tendrils of heat un-
curling from deep within the pit of her stomach. "I mean,
yes. Just a little...scattered."

Trace looked around the room, expecting to find it as disorganized as Cindy's mind obviously was. To his surprise everything was neatly packed and lined up by the door, ready to be taken to the Rover. Apparently she was eager to be gone from the forced intimacy of the small room and the implications of the single, lumpy mattress.

A thin smile grew beneath Trace's mustache. If Cindy thought the room was intimate, wait until she tried the Rover on for size. But he was no fool. He would say nothing. She could discover the dimensions of the Rover for herself.

Seven

The Rover hit a massive tree root, lurched, wallowed and thumped down the other side. Cindy opened her mouth to ask Trace if he was certain that the miserable track they were on was the road to San Juan de Whatsis. After an instant of deliberation, she closed her mouth again. Trace had been either surly or amused with her since the moment they had left the little room and he had calmly loaded everything into the Rover.

"Everything" had included one Cindy Ryan, who had been hustled into the vehicle with slightly less care than had been given to the bag of dirty clothes. Unlike the laundry, she had protested her treatment in a calm, firm voice. Trace had simply looked at her, called her princess and informed her that he had arranged for the Jeep to be driven back to Quito.

Cindy had been so stunned that she could think of nothing to say. She had remained silent since then. Trace had done the same, except for a few sizzling exceptions. One of

them occurred half an hour out of Popocaxtil, when a tire
went flat. There were many words then, all of them Trace's
and not a single one of them would have graced the ap-
proved list of a girl's finishing school. When Trace paused
for breath, Cindy spoke.

"Can I help?"

"With the swearing? I doubt it, princess," he said dryly.
"I know more languages than you do."

"With the tire," Cindy said, her voice tight.

"You sure can," he said as he slid out of the Rover. "You
can stay the hell out of my way."

The Rover's door slammed hard behind Trace. Cindy
hung on to her temper and settled in for a long wait.

As had happened many times since she had come to
Ecuador, she discovered that she had miscalculated. Despite the uneven, rutted, slippery ground, Trace had the bad
tire off and a new one in place within fifteen minutes.

"That was fast," Cindy said as Trace climbed back into
the Rover.

He grunted. "Anyone who can't change a tire has no
business on these roads."

"I changed a tire on the Jeep," Cindy retorted.

"Yeah. The right front."

"How did you know?" she asked, startled. The Jeep's
tires had been so caked with mud that there should have
been no way for Trace to tell which tire was new and which
was not.

"The lug nuts were so loose the wheel wobbled." Trace
turned and gave Cindy a glittering green glance. "You're
damned lucky that wheel didn't come off and dump you
over the edge of the pass," he said flatly. "It was a long,
long way down to the bottom, princess. Or was your nose
too high in the air to see the drop-off at your feet?"

Cindy looked at her hands clenched in her lap and said
nothing in her own defense, because there really was nothing for her to say. Trace was right: when it came to rough-

country skills, she had none. If he thought her stuck-up into the bargain, she could hardly object. She had been abrupt and impatient with him from the first instant she had seen him sprawled like a huge jungle cat in a warm corner of the Quito bar. His lean, relaxed, yet overwhelmingly male presence had done odd things to her nerves. She had taken it badly. Things had started going wrong between the two of them from that moment.

Blindly Cindy turned and stared out the window at the dense greenery that lurched by in time to the Rover's rough forward progress. *Maybe if I try hard enough, things can go right from now on. Maybe I can put my best foot forward and take the other one out of my mouth. Maybe then Trace will stop looking at me as if I'm just one more thing gone wrong with his life.*

Gradually the view outside the window resolved itself into separate shades of green reaching up toward a misty, pearl-white sky that was so brilliant it was impossible to look at directly. Leaves of all kinds unfurled to the white sky—leaves short and broad and glossy, leaves long and dark and swordlike, leaves lacy and graceful, blunt and leathery—more shapes and shades of green leaves than the human eye could distinguish or comprehend.

Without realizing it Cindy forgot her unhappy thoughts and became absorbed in the unfolding panorama of the land in a way that had been utterly impossible for her before, when she had been forced to give every bit of her attention to the road and the Jeep. Curious, wondering and finally awed, she began to understand the wild immensity of the country she had blithely taken on with no preparation beyond a dubious hand-drawn map and a rented Jeep of uncertain mechanical soundness.

In places along the narrow track the canopy of leaves closed tightly overhead, putting the road into total shade. In those places Cindy could see into the forest itself. Beneath the dense, leafy canopy, the forest floor was open. Too lit-

tle sunshine penetrated the layers of leaves for any but the
most shade-tolerant plants to survive beneath the tall trees.
Where the canopy had been torn by recent tree falls or by the
road itself, plants flourished in a solid green mass as they
fought a determined, silent, life-and-death struggle for a
place in the sun.

Despite the fact that the narrow road pitched up and
down as it wound over ridges and through what Cindy sus-
pected was a pass of sorts, the mountains themselves were
rarely visible. Part of the problem was the green canopy of
vegetation covering everything, muffling all sensory input,
all orientation, leaving at best only a vague sense of up and
down. Part of the visibility problem was stated in the name
of the landscape itself.

Cloud forest.

Moisture was the cloud forest's third dimension. Mist,
drizzle, windblown streamers of fog, water drops of all sizes
condensed on every green surface to make tiny clear beads
that gave off subtle glints of light when wind stirred through
the forest. And every bit of the moisture came from the
gently seething presence of grounded clouds. The mountains were dark, invisible sky castles more sensed than seen,
land swathed in silent, warm billows as though a giant had
exhaled against a mirror, blurring all reflections of reality.
Clouds were everywhere, permeating everything, even the
breaths that Cindy and Trace took.

Stretching from three thousand to eleven thousand feet
along the east-facing slopes of the Andes, the cloud forest
was bathed in perpetual moisture that came from thick,
sultry tropical air rising up mountain slopes, cooling and
condensing into clouds, and in the process creating a landscape that was like nothing else on earth. At times impenetrable, at times parklike, always expressed in shades of green
on green, infused with the silver rush of water, the cloud
forest lived and breathed, complete within its own immensity.

A searing torrent of language snapped Cindy out of her forest-induced reverie. The Rover lurched to a halt. She looked at Trace questioningly.

"Tire," he said in a clipped voice.

Automatically Cindy opened her mouth to ask if she could help, saw Trace's expectant, sardonic glance and closed her mouth once more, limiting her response to a nod. As the door slammed behind him, she looked at her watch. To her surprise, it was nearly noon. Her lips turned down in a rueful line at this latest underlining of her own incompetence relative to Trace's relentless skill. If she had been driving, the hours would have crawled far more slowly than the vehicle, and she would have been exhausted from wrestling with the steering wheel before she had come half so far.

Gloomily Cindy realized there was simply no doubt about it—traveling with Trace was much better in all ways than traveling by herself had been.

Not quite in all ways, she amended rebelliously. *When I was alone I could talk to myself. And better yet, I could get a civil answer!*

The Rover jiggled rhythmically as Trace jacked up the rear. Cindy glanced at her watch again and decided to risk Trace's wrath by rummaging for lunch. She knew there was something back in the cargo area. The smell of roast chicken and fresh corn tortillas was unmistakable.

Outside the Rover Trace pulled off the wheel, unstrapped the second spare he kept on the top of the Rover, and replaced the bad tire. He hesitated, then decided there was no help for it. He had to patch both ruined tubes on the two spares. If he didn't, sure as hell the next flat would come in a pouring rain on the edge of a road that would have given an eagle second thoughts.

Cursing steadily beneath his breath, Trace took the tire iron, levered both tires from the wheel rims, pulled out the tubes and went to work. In both cases the cause of the leak wasn't difficult to discover. Some of the forest trees were very hard. Fallen sticks or branches made very efficient spears, especially when lying concealed beneath a thin layer of mud or moss on top of the road. Usually he was lucky or skillful enough to avoid the hidden traps. Today his skill had been on hold too much of the time because his attention had been divided between the road and his beautiful, silent passenger.

As for his luck…it had been on a holiday since Quito and showed no signs of coming back anytime soon.

Trace heard the Rover's door open and shut. When Cindy didn't approach him, he assumed that she was going to venture into the forest for the obvious reason. He called out to her without looking up from his work on the tubes.

"Don't lose sight of the Rover. And watch out for plants like the one growing near the left front fender. The stems are hollow and are the home of some really vicious ants."

Cindy's answer was muffled but clearly nonrebellious, so Trace gave his attention back to the patches. He heard Cindy return, but she still didn't approach him. He finished checking the new patches on the tubes, put the tires back together and strapped them to their respective places on the top and rear of the Rover. He wiped down the tools and his own hands, topped off the gas tank, checked the water and decided everything would hold together until the next time he was looking at Cindy's profile when he damn well should have been looking at the road.

What the hell has she been thinking about? What's going on behind those beautiful black eyes? She hasn't said ten words since we left Popocaxtil.

Can you blame her? The last time she opened her mouth you landed on her with both feet.

If I had landed on her, it wouldn't have been with my feet. I've never made love to a woman in a car before, but better late than never, right?

Wrong. All wrong. Don't be any dumber than God made you. Get to Raul's place; show Cindy that Susan is okay; go tell Invers his problems with Big Eddy are solved and then start drinking until you forget the dark fire burning just beneath Cindy's lovely skin.

God, did she really shiver in my arms when I kissed her... or was it me shivering and wishing she wanted me?

Trace swore and tried to put Cindy out of his mind as he washed his hands beneath the trickling spout of the big water can attached to the rear bumper of the Rover. When he was finished he wiped his hands on his khakis and stretched. He was just thinking how wonderful a strong, hot cup of coffee would taste when he smelled the stuff of his dreams on the wind.

Inhaling, wondering if he were crazy, he followed the smell to the front of the Rover. The hood had been transformed into a table. Pieces of cold roast chicken and tortillas were laid out on top of a paper bag. Next to that was a mound of roughly hacked chunks of bittersweet chocolate. The food made his stomach growl in sudden demand, but it was the steaming mug that focused his attention. He reached for the mug, already anticipating the familiar, rich bite of coffee on his tongue.

"I didn't know if you took sugar or milk," Cindy said.

She glanced up from the road where she was crouched over a backpacker's stove that consisted of a single burner fueled by a canister of pressurized gas. A small pan of water was just coming to a boil. Next to her was another mug that wore what looked like a tin hat, which was actually the top half of a single-cup drip coffeepot. The mug itself provided the bottom half.

"This is fine. Much more than I expected," Trace added between sips of the scalding brew. He made a sound of satisfaction. "Good and strong, too. The way I like it."

Cindy smiled in relief. "I wasn't sure about how to use your little half pot," she admitted, "but the color of that first cup looked right. Rye taught me to make it strong enough to stand up to a high-country blizzard."

Trace grunted, suddenly less pleased with the coffee. He couldn't help wondering what other ways Rye had taught Cindy to please a man.

"He even taught me to like drinking it," Cindy continued as she poured water into the tiny pot perched over her mug.

She glanced over her shoulder, hoping that Trace had accepted the coffee as it had been meant—as a peace overture. A single look at his hard features told her that coffee hadn't been enough to get the job done. Unconsciously biting her lip, she turned back to her own coffee. By the time her cup was ready, Trace had finished his. When he put his mug aside to reach for tortillas, she substituted her fresh cup for his empty one and set up the coffee maker once more.

In quiet horror Cindy watched while Trace tucked chunks of chocolate and chicken into a tortilla, rolled it up and ate it with every evidence of pleasure. She had meant the chocolate as dessert, not as part of the main course.

"It all ends up in the same place, princess," Trace said sardonically, accurately reading the look on her face.

Cindy's lips turned down at the nickname she had come to hate.

He smiled thinly. He knew that she didn't like being called princess. That was why he did it. That, and to remind himself that she was the spoiled child of wealth, even if she would rather die than admit it to him.

You know, you really should quit riding her with the princess routine, Trace advised himself. *You're not supposed to know who she is, remember? As for you being angry because she doesn't trust you enough to tell you her real name—she'd be a fool if she went around announcing her wealth and you know it. South America is a close second to Italy as the kidnap capital of the world. That's why Invers was sweating bullets at the thought of having Big Eddy's daughter waltzing around the cloud forest looking for another ditzy, ritzy American woman.*

On the other hand, pointed out the devil's advocate that lived within Trace, *if Cindy hates the nickname princess so much, all she has to do is ask me not to use it. Just ask me. That's all. No big deal.*

Except to her.

And to me, Trace admitted silently. *If it's the last thing she does on this green earth, she'll ask me for something. Anything.*

And I'll give it to her, no matter what it is or who it costs.

With his coffee cup Trace drank a silent toast to his vow. Only after he had swallowed did it register on his mind that the formerly empty cup had been magically refilled. He looked at the mug and then at Cindy, who was just pouring a final measure of water through the tiny pot. He realized that she had given him her cup.

Maybe she drank some while I was cleaning up.

"You like this blend?" Trace asked, inhaling the fragrance rising from his mug.

"Tell you after I've had a sip," Cindy said, blowing across the steaming surface of her coffee. "But if this is what I think it is, I love it."

Trace started to say something, then stopped. It gave him an odd feeling in the pit of his stomach to realize that she had given him two cups of coffee before she had taken so much as a taste for herself. That wasn't what he would have expected from a child of wealth, especially from one who was too proud to even ask him for the time of day.

But then, Cindy had been unexpected from the start, and in very uncomfortable ways.

"Wonderful," she murmured, closing her eyes as the taste of coffee spread through her in a fragrant, revitalizing wave. "Just as I remembered from my last birthday. Beans so mellow you could eat them."

"You're sure this is the same coffee?"

"Positive. I almost cried when I used up what Dad had sent me."

"Then your father must know somebody who knows Raul."

"Who?"

"Raul Almeda. This is his private blend, grown from his own coffee plants and given to his friends and business partners. Raul owns a vast *hacienda* up ahead that runs from the lowlands to the cloud forest." Very casually Trace added, "If Susan isn't at the next village, doubtless she'll be with Raul, her feet on an embroidered stool and servants hovering to grant her every wish."

"Sounds boring," Cindy retorted.

"Only to people who have been rich enough, for long enough, to know what it's like. Most never get the chance to find out. But you wouldn't know about that, would you?"

"Would it make any difference if I did?"

Trace's mouth turned up at one corner in a smile that was as cold as his eyes. "I doubt it, princess. Money just doesn't get some jobs done, and they're nearly always the jobs worth doing."

Cindy made no response this time. What Trace had said was a razor truth that she had encountered too many times not to acknowledge it, and each time she confronted it the truth sliced deeper. Money simply couldn't buy the important things. It couldn't buy self-respect or intelligence or talent or real companionship or laughter or . . . love.

Love was most definitely one thing money could not buy. Nor could begging. Love was a gift freely given.

But nobody gave gifts to Big Eddy's daughter.

Eight

Cindy watched Trace turn away from the natives he had been questioning. He reached the Rover in a few swift steps, slid in behind the wheel and slammed the door just as the overcast condensed into an odd, dense mist.

"Susan left a few days ago, just before the first hard storm," Trace said. "She was hitching a ride with one of Raul's workers."

Biting her lip, Cindy stared out the side window, not wanting to reveal her worry to Trace.

"Don't look so glum. Raul's *hacienda* is just a few hours down the road. When it started pouring, I'll bet they just made a run for one of the hunting cabins Raul has scattered up and down the mountainside. They're fully stocked at all times for just such emergencies."

"Do they have phones?"

"The cabins? Hardly. Despite the greenery, princess, this isn't Central Park."

"Really? What an astonishing revelation," Cindy said before she could stop herself. She really did hate that nickname.

"It might be a revelation if you'd think about what it means instead of making smart remarks. No phones means no way to call and tell people you're all right. That's what the Andean cloud forest is all about. Lack of communication."

"Precisely. If something went wrong for her—"

"Quit borrowing trouble," Trace snarled, letting out the clutch and leaving the village behind. "We've got enough of our own without you hunting for more."

Before Cindy could ask what Trace meant, the swirling mist surrounding the Rover changed into true rain.

In the next hours Cindy came to understand rain and Trace Rawlings in a new way. She passed from nervousness to disbelief to admiration and finally to outright awe as she watched Trace negotiate the narrow, melting, liquefying road. She wouldn't have made it half a kilometer out of San Juan de Whatsis and she knew it. It took experience, strength, coordination and coolness to hold the slewing, sliding, slithering Rover to the course. Time after time Trace guided and bullied the vehicle through situations where Cindy knew she would have ended up sideways or topside down or hopelessly mired. Even if she had managed to extricate herself and the Rover, she knew she would have just ended up in trouble all over again a few yards down the road.

If you could call it a road. She no longer did. It was a pathway to hell; a slippery, sliding, greasy brown string unwinding endlessly downward beneath clinging slate veils and between blackish green walls of vegetation that thrashed like souls in torment. Gray rain hammered down from the heavens without pause or purpose, reminding men of just how the oceans had come to cover three-quarters of the planet.

Cindy lost count of the times Trace dragged a winch cable into the forest, wrapped the cable around a suitable tree and yanked the Rover out of a mud hole. She lost track of the passage of time as well, and of distance, and of all directions except down.

Despite the rain and the wind, the air wasn't cold. It wasn't even cool. That made sense to Cindy in a crazy way. Hell, after all, was reputed to be warm, and she had no doubt that hell must be where they were headed, slithering endlessly downward, a descent that was underlined by the tropical heat of the air, a viscous warmth that deprived her of any temperature sense at all. Everything she touched seemed to hold the same amount of heat—the window, the upholstery, the rain, her own body.

Numbly Cindy watched as Trace got out in order to investigate a low spot in the road on foot. Being alone further increased her sense of unreality, of being suspended within the endless, elemental drumroll of water that was battering the Rover. Her body was tense and her throat ached out of a futile desire to somehow lighten Trace's burden. Without Trace she would have been helpless, and she knew it to the marrow of her bones.

The realization neither frightened nor irritated Cindy. It was simply a fact like rain or mud or a cloud forest that bowed to no man.

Even Trace Rawlings.

"That's it," he said flatly, climbing into the Rover and turning off the engine.

Cindy blinked as though coming out of a trance. "We're there?"

"If by 'there' you mean Raul's *hacienda*, no. If 'there' means where we're going to spend the rest of the storm, yes. There's no point in pushing anymore. At this rate we won't reach the *hacienda* before midnight. We'd make much better time going on foot."

"Oh." Cindy peered through the windshield, trying to see where they were. All she saw was rain. Not that it mattered. If Trace said they couldn't go any farther, then they couldn't, period.

"No argument?" he asked sardonically.

Cindy shook her head. "Frankly I don't see where you got the strength to go this far."

"That's easy enough. I didn't want to be trapped for the night with you in the Rover." Trace shrugged. "But here we are anyway."

"Trapped," she repeated, her mouth turning down.

If Cindy had had any doubt about how Trace regarded her, he had just removed it. He had driven for hours over impossible roads in the hope of avoiding the opportunity to spend the night with her again.

Trace saw the unhappy line of Cindy's mouth and said coldly, "Don't worry, I—"

"Yes, I know," she interrupted bitterly. "You won't stick your hand up my blouse while I'm asleep."

Don't bet anything important on it, princess. I want you like hell on fire. That's why I kept driving long after I knew it was a lost cause. I hoped I'd be too tired to get hard every time I looked at you.

It didn't work.

For the sake of his own pride, however, Trace kept his thoughts to himself. Besides, what woman would put up with a man who was covered with mud and smelled as if he had carried the Rover on his back for the past three hours? In fact, Trace was surprised Cindy hadn't complained about him once through the long afternoon. He could barely stand himself in the confines of the Rover.

"I'm going to take a shower," he said abruptly.

"What? Where?"

Trace's laugh was a bark of disbelief. "You've got to be kidding."

Cindy looked at the warm rain pouring down and understood. She watched while Trace stretched over the seat of the Rover and snagged his shaving kit. It was an easy reach for him because there was no back seat. As had been the case with the Jeep, the Rover's rear seat had been taken out to make more room for carrying equipment and supplies.

After Trace vanished into the rain with a bar of soap in his hand, Cindy rolled down both front windows for ventilation. The rain blowing inside didn't worry her. Trace had been in and out of the Rover so often that everything that could get wet already was. She unclipped the cargo net, crawled over the seat back and began assembling ingredients for dinner.

Given the single burner and the impossibility of cooking outside, Cindy didn't try for anything elaborate. Fresh coffee was first on the list. While the water came to a boil she diced up a small tin of ham and added water to a packet of sliced freeze-dried potatoes. More water went into a mixture that purported to be freeze-dried carrots and peas. Another bar of chocolate turned up. She hid it, afraid that Trace would add it to the stew she was assembling. By the time Trace returned from his makeshift shower, Cindy had made a canteen of coffee, cooked the ham and vegetables together and steamed the remaining tortillas into a renewed flexibility.

"Here," she said, kneeling on the front seat and leaning over into the cargo area until she could grab a mug. Quickly she poured coffee from the canteen and handed the mug to Trace. "The rest of it will be ready in a few minutes."

Wordlessly Trace took the mug. He stared at the darkly reflective surface of the coffee as though he were looking into the future. It was safer than staring at Cindy. In the process of getting the food ready, she had gone close enough to the open windows for rain to dampen odd patches of her clothes. When she leaned over the seat, those wet spots stuck to the curves beneath. When she turned around and sat facing the windshield, her blouse clung to her nipples as though dampened by a lover's mouth.

With an inarticulate curse, Trace forced himself to think about something else. Anything else. Counting raindrops, for instance. Licking them from her body one by one...

"Ready?" Cindy asked.

Trace turned and gave her a smoldering green glance. With a sinking heart Cindy wondered if he would be in a better mood after he had eaten. Silently she handed him a plate of food. She knew it wasn't haute cuisine, but she thought it deserved better than the black scowl he gave it. For several minutes the only sound was that of the rain and the muffled scrape of tin spoons over tin plates.

"More coffee?" she asked finally.

Trace held out his mug. "Yes." Then, softly. "Thank you."

Startled, Cindy looked up from the canteen and smiled. "You're welcome, Trace."

Her smile and the sound of his name on her lips sent streamers of dark fire through Trace's body. Suddenly he knew he couldn't spend another moment in the Rover's enforced intimacy without making a very hard pass at Cindy. That didn't bother him as much as the angry realization that he didn't know what he would do if she turned him down.

And he had every expectation that she would do just that.

"Look," Cindy said, turning toward the window. "It's stopped raining. Well, almost. It's not raining nearly so much."

Trace's head turned. Cindy was right. As suddenly as the hard rain had begun, it had stopped. The end of the downpour was too late to do the road much good, however. Dark would come long before the low places had drained. There seemed to be no help for it—in the next few hours he would get the excruciating opportunity of discovering how long he could hold out before he made a fool of himself, or worse, with Cindy.

A pale flash against the dark green of the forest caught Trace's eye. Slowly he made out a series of blazes on the trunk of one of the bigger trees. Once he had spotted the first blaze he had no trouble at all deciphering the message Raul's workers had hacked with machetes into the tree's trunk. He and Cindy were at the edge of one of Raul's forestry experiments. A few hundred yards down the hill there should be a clear trail used by Raul's men. A few klicks up the trail—straight up—would be the spur road leading to the big house, the main Almeda residence.

And in that residence there would be more than enough rooms to separate two unexpected guests. Trace wouldn't have to see Cindy, much less be forced constantly to brush against her.

Trace finished off his coffee in a gulp. "As soon as you're done eating, we'll walk to Raul's house."

Cindy looked blank. "Walk?"

His eyes narrowed. "That's right, princess. Walk. It's a form of transportation often used by the peons of the world."

It took a considerable effort, but Cindy managed not to say anything more inflammatory than "Is it far?"

"A few klicks as the crow goes. Four or five times that by the road. We'll leave the luggage here. When the road dries out a bit, Raul's men will bring the Rover to the big house."

Without a word Cindy finished her coffee, gathered up the dirty dishes and pushed against the unlatched passenger door. Trace started to protest that she would get wet in the steady drizzle, then realized how foolish that would sound. She was going to get a lot wetter on the way to the big house.

It would make more sense to stay here, Trace told himself.

The hell it would, he snarled in silent, instant response. *I'd be all over her like hot rain.*

Like I said. It would make more sense to stay here.

The door of the Rover slammed behind Trace. Before
Cindy could protest he had taken the dishes from her and
shoved her purse into her hands. He fired the dishes into the
back of the Rover, yanked his machete from the sheath at
his waist and stalked toward the blazed tree, hoping that
Raul's men had left some encroaching forest for him to hack
up.

After a few moments Cindy followed Trace. There was no
path, but the walking wasn't too difficult at first. They were
in one of the densely shaded, almost parklike areas of the
cloud forest. The only thing she had to watch out for were
tree roots and moss. By placing her feet carefully, but
quickly, she could keep up with Trace. Barely.

Just as Cindy was congratulating herself on her previ-
ously unsuspected wilderness skills, her foot slipped on a
mossy root and she sat down hard. Hoping that Trace
hadn't noticed, she scrambled to her feet and wiped off her
palms on her colorful pants, leaving the first of what would
be many such smears.

Beyond the blazed tree a trail of sorts appeared. The
footing varied between slick and impossible. Cindy found
herself grabbing at branches and bark, bushes and droop-
ing vines, anything to help her keep her balance on the narrow path. Most of the time she stayed upright. The rest of
the time she gathered new marks for her clothes and body.

Mist closed in again, swathing everything in hushed
moisture. Trace was too busy hacking at intrusive greenery
to notice that Cindy was barely managing to keep up with
him. He moved forward with the steady, rhythmic body
motions of a strong man who was accustomed to the cloud
forest's demands. From time to time he glanced over his
shoulder to check on Cindy, but could see little more of her
than a dark shape veiled in the mist of a grounded cloud.

Halfway up the very steep path he paused, looked over his
shoulder and saw no one. He called out and was answered
by a muffled voice. He started to ask Cindy if the pace was

too fast, then stopped himself. If he was going too fast, surely she would have the sense to say something. Wouldn't she?

Sure. Right after she finished teaching stubborn to a Missouri mule.

"Everything all right?" Trace asked, cursing himself even as he spoke.

"Just fine," Cindy said through gritted teeth as she pulled herself upright with the aid of the same tree root that had tripped her in the first place.

Trace hesitated, not liking the breathless quality of Cindy's voice. He checked his watch. If they were going to get to the big house by dark, they had to keep going.

"Let me know if you have to stop," Trace said.

Cindy made a sound that Trace took as a response. With a last look over his shoulder, he turned back to the trail that had only recently been hacked from the cloud forest's solid green body. Unconsciously he resumed the unhurried, unbroken rhythm of chop and walk, chop and walk, chop and walk. Trace made it look effortless, but the skill with which he moved through the dense forest was the result of hard experience and an even harder body.

Only when the new forest trail cut the spur road to the *hacienda* did Trace stop. As he stood quietly, breathing deeply and easily, he realized that he had fallen into a pace that might have been rewarding for him but almost certainly had been too hard on a proud princess.

"Cindy?"

No answer came back from the swirling streamers of cloud.

"Cindy!"

There was no response.

Even before the sound of his call was absorbed into the forest's silence, Trace was back on the narrow path, moving with doubled speed, cursing.

Cindy heard Trace coming toward her long before she saw him condense out of the gray-white mist swathing the steep, rough trail. The last thing she wanted was for Trace to find her sprawled out flat on her face, compliments of a tree root she would have sworn leaped up to grab her foot. Hurriedly she tried to claw her way to her feet, but succeeded only in losing her balance once more. Doggedly she pushed herself to her hands and knees.

Trace stopped and stared at the apparition that was kneeling before him in the narrow trail. Relief and anger warred for possession of his tongue. Anger won.

"What the hell do you think you're doing?" he demanded.

Cindy had no problem with conflicting emotions. Her peace overtures toward Trace had been singularly unsuccessful. That left war.

"Worshipping the ground you walk on," she retorted. "What the hell does it look like?"

Unfortunately for her intentions, Cindy sounded more worn out than sarcastic, and she knew it. She set her teeth and started to pull herself upright again, hating her own weakness, hating Trace for seeing it, hating herself for caring, for wanting to see something besides impatience and anger in Trace's eyes when he looked at her.

Trace hissed a curse through his teeth and reached out to help Cindy to her feet.

"Don't touch me."

Trace was close enough to see the utter fury of defeat in Cindy's black eyes. She was like a cornered animal turning on its tormentor. Pain lanced through him, drawing his face into bleak lines. He hadn't meant to do this to her. Why in the name of God couldn't she even open her mouth and ask him for what she needed?

"I'm not a bloody mind reader! Why didn't you ask me to slow down or stop?" Trace demanded harshly. And then his expression became even more grim as he heard his own question. "Dumb question, right? I keep forgetting. You'd rather die than ask a peon for the time of day. Better watch it, princess. You just might get your wish."

With a single quick motion Trace sheathed his machete. Another even quicker motion brought his hands around Cindy's upper arms. In an instant he had lifted her to her feet.

"Now, if you had *asked* me not to touch you, I wouldn't lay a finger on you," Trace said in a clipped voice. "But you didn't ask. You did what came naturally. You ordered. A princess to the marrow of your elegant bones. Would you like to ask this peon not to touch you? Nicely?"

The surge of rage that had come to Cindy when Trace had once again found her grubbing in the mud faded, leaving nothing behind but defeat. She turned her face away from him and said nothing.

"That's what I thought," Trace said, disgusted with her and with himself for caring that Cindy disliked him so much that she wouldn't ask him for anything, no matter how much she might need it. He pointed her toward the trail. "Walk. I'll be right behind you."

Cindy started up the trail. Three steps later she would have fallen flat had it not been for Trace's left hand closing around her upper arm in the instant after she slipped. He held her upright until her feet found stable footing once more. When she tripped again a few steps later, he grabbed her again. This time he didn't release her. On the steepest parts of the trail he shifted his grip to her bottom, boosting her along as she scrambled forward. When they came to the muddy spur road that led to the Almeda home, Trace moved up alongside Cindy so that his left hand could keep a firm grip on her right arm.

They were still walking that way when Raul and Susan found them.

Nine

"Susan! Is it really you? Are you all right?" Cindy asked in a rush, hardly able to believe her eyes when she saw the stunning, cinnamon-haired woman sitting at ease in a Jeep.

"You just stole my lines," Susan said, looking at Cindy with real concern. "What in God's name happened to you? Did you have an accident?"

Cindy looked at her friend, who was immaculate in an ice-blue silk jumpsuit that perfectly matched her gorgeous eyes. Then Cindy looked at herself. Her unstructured clothes had long since passed beyond the point of fashionable disarray. They were wet, ripped and stained by mud and vegetation to the point that their predominant color was an unappetizing greenish brown.

Cindy started to explain what had happened but the words wedged in her throat. She had just caught a view of Trace from the corner of her eye. He was staring at Susan as though transfixed. It wasn't the first time Cindy had seen a man respond that way to Susan. It was the first time it had hurt, however.

"Ask Tarzan," Cindy said curtly.

"Tarzan?" Unerringly Susan's wide blue eyes turned toward Trace. "It does rather fit, doesn't it?"

Trace's smile was a scimitar curve in his hard face. "I told you Susan was all right, princess. Raul's very good with women. Aren't you, Raul?"

For the first time Cindy focused on the man sitting in the driver's seat of the Jeep. Her eyes widened fractionally. Raul's hair was silky blond. His skin was a rich, dark gold and his eyes were as black as her own. It was a startling combination, particularly when set against the bold, very masculine bone structure of his face.

Rather cynically Trace watched Cindy's reaction to Raul. She wouldn't be the first woman to fall at Raul's feet after taking one look. Nor would she be the last. That didn't mean that Trace had to enjoy watching it. Somehow he had thought Cindy would have better sense than to be knocked over by a man's looks. God knows she had managed to ignore his own looks without difficulty, and more than one woman had told Trace he was handsome. Not Cindy, though. Not by so much as a sideways glance. The only passion she showed when she looked at him was a desire to commit mayhem on his much stronger body.

"You must be *Señor* Almeda," Cindy said. "I'm Cindy Ryan, Susan's partner."

Raul's jet-black eyes widened as he looked at the rumpled, muddy, thoroughly disheveled creature in front of him. "It is a great pleasure, *Señorita* Ryan," he said. "Susan has told me much about you."

"I left out her enthusiasm for mud baths," Susan said, her eyes still disbelieving. Then she added, "You really are all right, aren't you?"

"Nothing a hot bath and a decent bed won't cure."

"But of course," Raul said instantly. "Please, get in the Jeep."

"Thought you'd never ask," Trace said dryly. Before Cindy could object, he picked her up and dumped her in the back seat of the open Jeep.

"We were just checking on the bridge over Orchid Ravine," Raul explained as he drove down the muddy road.

"And?" Trace asked.

"I would not want to attempt the bridge at the moment," Raul said carefully.

Trace grunted and flashed a jungle-green glance at Susan, who was smiling at Raul. Silently Trace conceded that if Cindy were watching him the way Susan was watching Raul, Trace wouldn't be in any hurry to rush his bridges back into civilization, either.

"Then it looks like you're stuck with us for a day or two," Trace said. "We walked overland on the new trail your men cut up the far side of Thousand Springs Divide."

"We? *Señorita* Ryan was with you?" Raul asked, startled.

"Every step of the way."

"*La pobrecita,*" murmured Raul. "Poor little one. I am a man, yet I would not wish to make that walk with you."

Cindy smiled wanly. "Trace wasn't wild about the idea of having me underfoot, either."

Raul's laugh was low, husky, intimate. "I doubt that very much. My friend has never turned down the company of a charming and beautiful woman."

Just as Cindy found herself warming to the compliment, common sense intervened. At the moment she was about as beautiful as a handful of mud, and as charming, too.

"It is very kind of you to say so," Cindy murmured, "even though it's a gigantic whopper."

"What is this 'gigantic whopper'?" Raul asked.

"A big lie," Trace said succinctly.

Raul blinked, then laughed again. "Now I believe you are truly Cindy Ryan."

"Tongue like a wasp," Trace agreed.

"The hotter the sting, the sweeter the honey," Raul said, smiling with distinct masculine satisfaction.

Cindy bit her tongue and said nothing. Susan winked at her and began fishing for information with all the subtlety of an old, trusted friend.

"What are you doing out here? And how did you end up with Trace?"

"I came to find you. Trace is helping me."

"Why?"

"Because I'm paying him," Cindy retorted.

"Puh-leese," Susan said, calling upon the mist as her witness to Cindy's recalcitrance. "I meant why did you come after me? Didn't you get my note telling you my change of plans?"

"That was nearly two weeks ago. I was . . . worried."

Susan made a humming sound that managed to sound skeptical and musical at the same time. "Translated that means you left because Rye and Lisa were busy making another baby and Big Eddy was running around trying to buy studs for you again."

"Susan!" Cindy said, appalled.

"What? You know as well as I do that he offered the last hotshot a ten thousand dollar bonus if he got you pregnant. You see," Susan said kindly to Trace, "her father just recently figured out that a woman only needs a man to get pregnant. Marriage isn't necessary. Even more pertinent, if Cindy doesn't marry, her children will have her last name, which is also Big Eddy's. He was quite pleased by the discovery, because he wants a raft of grandchildren, and he's going to have them if he has to kill his own children trying. Do you blame Cindy for telling the old bulldozer to go to hell and running after me instead?"

"Oh my God," Cindy said faintly, putting her face in her hands without regard for the bits of vegetation still clinging to her fingers.

Trace looked from Susan to Cindy. He picked over the information for the least incriminating parts. "Rye and Lisa, huh? Is she the one who beat you to it?" Trace asked.

"To what? Pregnancy?" Susan asked when it became apparent that Cindy wasn't going to answer Trace. "There was no contest. Lisa and Rye wanted kids."

"And Cindy didn't?" Trace asked.

"She's old-fashioned. She wanted a husband first."

"What was wrong with Rye?"

"Same parents, that's what. He's her brother."

Trace digested that. "Oh."

"She sicced me on Rye once, but it was too late," Susan continued. "He'd already seen Lisa."

Raul smiled. "I can't imagine that would make a difference once he saw you, *corazon*."

"You haven't seen Lisa," Susan and Cindy said as one.

"She's small, delicate, has eyes the color of amethysts and natural platinum hair down to her hips," Susan continued, ticking off Lisa's attributes. "And innocent. God above, she was innocent! She'd been raised with the kind of tribes you only see in National Geographic specials."

"I should have sent Lisa after you," Cindy said softly. "Anyone who can make a wicked knife from an antler and a piece of glass would be right at home in the cloud forest. She would have been a help to Trace, not a burden."

"I am sure you were not a burden," Raul said instantly.

"You're very kind," Cindy said, closing her eyes. She smiled sadly. "I'm sure if it had been you doing the guiding, I wouldn't have felt like a burden. But I would have been a burden just the same."

Susan gave her friend a worried look, then glanced toward Trace. He looked back at her with opaque green eyes.

"You're just tired, Cinderella," Susan said gently, leaning over the seat and stroking Cindy's wet, tangled hair. "The world will look different after you're dry and clean and rested."

Cindy made a noise that could have been agreement, but from the down-turned line of her mouth, Trace doubted that she meant it. Frowning, Susan examined her friend's wan face and closed eyes before she turned around and stared out the windshield again.

A few minutes later the Jeep hit a bump. Cindy didn't open her eyes as a lock of her hair fell forward across her face. With gentle fingers Trace stroked the hair back behind her ear. When she didn't move at all, he realized that she had fallen asleep. Just as the Jeep hit another bump, he reached out and lifted her half across his lap. When she mumbled a question that was also a name, Trace knew what to say.

"Yes, it's Rye. Go to sleep, Cindy. Everything's all right."

Susan's head snapped around. Trace looked back at her with eyes that were as green and as impenetrable as the cloud forest itself. One big hand stroked Cindy's hair slowly, gently, while the other hand held her against his chest. Cindy murmured something and burrowed more deeply into Trace's arms.

After a moment Susan spoke.

"When her mother died, Cindy was just a kid. Rye used to hear her crying in the middle of the night. He'd go and hold her until she fell asleep again."

Trace's eyelids flinched but he said nothing.

"What did you do to her?" Susan asked flatly.

"Nothing major. I'm a lousy mind reader, so I tried to teach Cindy to ask for what she needs. That's all."

"That's all?" Susan's eyes widened into deep, faintly tilted pools of blue. "She never asks anyone for anything. Ever. Not me. Not God. Not even Rye. But she'll give you the heart from her body if she thinks you need it...or if you ask her for it,'' Susan added.

Trace's mouth curled into a thin, sardonic smile. "The only thing she'd willingly give me is a knife between the ribs.''

"That doesn't sound like Cindy."

"Maybe you don't know her as well as you thought."

"And maybe I do," Susan retorted. "If you managed to get under Cindy's skin deep enough to get her angry, congratulations. No man has raised her temperature a quarter of a degree since a walking disaster called Jason came into her life. You would have gotten along fine with Jason.''

Trace raised a single eyebrow in skeptical query.

"Like you," Susan said coolly, "Jason believed in making Cindy beg for every little thing from a hamburger to a good-night kiss.''

Have you ever had to beg? Well, I have and I'll never do it again.

"There is one hell of a difference between asking and begging,'' Trace said between his clenched teeth, as though it were Cindy rather than Susan he was trying to convince.

"Try explaining that to Cindy."

"I did."

"Didn't work, did it?"

"No."

"But you didn't give up, did you?" Susan continued icily, looking at Cindy's pale face, her skin drawn by fatigue even in sleep. "You just kept hammering away at her until you beat her down. Like I said. You and dear, sweet Jason have a lot in common.''

"Corazon," murmured Raul. "Trace is not like that."

"Not to you, surely," Susan said. "You'd take his head off and make an orchid planter of it.''

"You underestimate Trace," Raul said dryly. "And you misunderstand him, as well.''

"Said the crocodile's brother to the curious little fish,"
Susan muttered in disgust. "The only reason a croc has a
mouthful of teeth is so he can smile real pretty, right?"

Trace smiled.

Susan threw her hands up and didn't say anything else
until the Jeep stopped in front of a stately, multistoried
house that grew elegantly in the midst of the cloud forest.
Cindy stirred. Reluctantly Trace eased her over onto the
seat. Without waiting for anyone else to get out, he vaulted
over the side of the vehicle. When a woman's broad, smiling face appeared at the front door, Trace called out in rapid
Spanish mixed with hissing, harsh *indio* words. The big
woman laughed and returned the bear hug Trace was giving her.

Susan sighed. "I take it that Trace is a friend of the family?"

"He is a member of the family," Raul corrected, smiling. "My cousin."

"Ah, the wonderful taste of raw foot in the mouth."

"I beg your pardon?"

"Never mind," Susan said, pushing a long strand of cinnamon hair aside. "I still think he was too hard on Cindy."

"So does he."

Susan looked startled. Before she could think of anything to say, Trace had returned.

"Tia says we can clean up and eat dinner here, but then
I'm to take the Jeep and Cindy to my cabin."

Raul's eyebrows arched upward in an exact echo of
Trace's dark ones. "You're not to sleep here?"

"No." Smiling, Trace switched to Spanish. "Tia wants
you to have more time to get to know your...guest. Better
watch it, cousin. Tia is already making up wedding lists in
her mind."

An irritated expression darkened Raul's handsome features. Then he shrugged and answered in Spanish. "As al-

ways, with Tia it is easier to be as the forest and bend beneath the wind, yes?''

"You always were more successful at bending than I was, *compadre*,'' agreed Trace. He leaned into the Jeep, lifted Cindy into his arms and switched to English. "Wake up, princess, or get kissed by a frog.''

"That's not how the fairy tale went,'' Cindy complained sleepily, turning her face into Trace's neck.

He closed his eyes as he felt the accidental brush of her lips against his skin. It was all he could do to control a shudder of violent response.

"That's the thing about life,'' he said huskily. "It's always so damned unexpected.''

For instance, he hadn't expected to be spending another night alone with Cindy. In fact, he'd dragged her up half a mountain just to avoid the prospect . . . only to find himself booked into the fragrant, hushed silence of the Cloud Cabin. One man. One woman. One bed.

"One hell of a mess,'' he muttered.

A night on the hard floor had never looked so unappealing.

Cindy looked from the inky wall of forest rising on either side of the Jeep to the black shadows thrown across Trace's face by the dashboard lights. Neither moon nor stars were visible overhead. Mist seethed in silver streamers through the bright shafts of illumination given off by the Jeep's headlights.

"It's not much farther,'' Trace said.

His tone was like the line of his mouth. Flat, hard, unyielding. Cindy sighed. Apparently he was angry at not being allowed to stay at the big house.

"Don't blame Raul,'' she said hesitantly. "He couldn't have known we were coming, so he could hardly be expected to prepare rooms for us.''

Trace gave Cindy a sardonic, sideways glance. "Rooms are always prepared. Raul just needed time to be alone with Susan. He wants her."

"So does every other man who's ever seen her."

"I don't."

"Yeah. Right. That's why you looked at her like you'd never seen a woman before." Suddenly Cindy laughed, remembering how she herself must have looked a few hours before. "Or not for a few days, anyway," she added.

Cindy looked down at herself and grimaced. She was wearing one of Susan's outfits. The fitted blouse and mid-calf cotton-knit skirt looked smashing on Susan. Cindy, however, had more inches around the bust and hips than her willowy friend. The skirt fit in the waist and was the right length. The same could be said of the blouse. After that the only thing that could be said was that the outfit covered everything required by law.

In all, Cindy felt like a sausage stuffed into somebody else's skin. Every time she took a breath she was reminded of Susan's slender, elegant figure—and of her own, less-than-slender self.

"Fishing for compliments again?"

Cindy's bittersweet smile vanished. She didn't say another word, even when Trace stopped the Jeep long enough to put on its canvas top. The silence grew oppressive long before the Jeep's headlights picked out a small cabin tucked away just at the edge of darkness, bathed in mist and the warm silver rain that had just begun to fall. The sound of water running over the Jeep's canvas roof was soothing, almost caressing.

With a corner of her mind, Cindy wondered how Trace had known that it would rain before they reached the cabin. It was just one more of the many ways in which Trace had proven himself to be supremely at home in the cloud forest. And with each of those proofs Cindy herself had become more defensive, more determined to demonstrate to him that she wasn't simply a burden to be hauled through the wilderness like two piglets squealing in a burlap sack.

But she was a burden. It hurt to admit it, yet it was the simple truth.

Trace pulled up close to the cabin, switched to parking lights and turned off the Jeep's engine.

"In order to save a big scene when you walk into the cabin," Trace said in a clipped voice, "I'll tell you three things right now. One: there's only one bed. Two: you're sleeping in it. Three: I'll sleep on the floor or in the Jeep, whichever I decide is more comfortable."

Cindy tried to think of something to say. Nothing came to her but the intense, unhappy realization that Trace would spend a very uncomfortable night because of her.

"That isn't necessary," she said quietly. "We could share the bed. I know you don't want...that is, you wouldn't..."

"Stick my hand up your blouse?" Trace offered in a cold voice.

Cindy made a helpless gesture. She knew that she didn't appeal to Trace sexually, but she hadn't wanted to state it quite so baldly.

"Exactly," she said, taking a deep breath. "I know you don't want me so there's no reason not to..." Her voice died as she looked into Trace's narrowed, bleak eyes and the savage lines of his face. "I'm doing this badly, aren't I? Trace, I'm not strong enough to carry you off to a comfortable bed after you fall asleep." She took a deep breath and said quickly, "I never even thanked you for that, or for all the other things you've done for me. I should have thanked you. I wanted to. I just...couldn't. Thanking you would have meant admitting that I couldn't have done it by myself, that I needed you. And years ago I swore I would never need anyone again."

The sad, rueful sound of Cindy's laughter made Trace ache to take her in his arms, but he didn't move toward her.

If he touched her he was afraid he wouldn't stop with simple comfort. He wanted her until he could barely breathe.

"But I do need you," Cindy continued. "I'm way out of my depth in the cloud forest. I need you the way I've never needed anyone. It's a terrible burden for you to be needed like that and it's very uncomfortable for me. I didn't handle it well at all. You see, I've been fighting my own battles for years, and losing them when it came to that. Alone."

Cindy made another futile gesture with her hand and then rolled down the passenger window, wanting to touch the rain. The lights of the dashboard illuminated her face and turned the water drops washing over her outstretched hand into molten gold. She brought her fingertips to her lips and delicately licked up the glittering moisture.

"Sweet," she murmured absently. "Why does that always surprise me?"

Trace clenched his jaw against the raw sound of need that had risen in his throat. Her spontaneous, utterly natural sensuality was killing him and she didn't even know it.

"What I'm trying to say," Cindy continued, holding her hand out in the rain once more, watching warm liquid gather and run down her fingers, "is that I'm sorry I was a burden to you. On the way back to Quito, I promise I'll be better at staying out of your way. As for tonight, there's no good reason that we can't share the bed."

"You are dead wrong."

Trace's dark, gritty voice was so close that Cindy turned toward him in surprise.

"What?"

"This," he said harshly.

Trace's shoulders eclipsed the dashboard lights at the same instant that his powerful hands framed Cindy's face. His mouth came down hard over hers, twisting urgently, and his tongue shot into the warm feminine darkness he had been aching to penetrate. For a long minute that was just what he did, repeatedly, claiming her mouth with a search-

ing intimacy that made her tremble. And then she realized
that Trace was trembling, too.

Trace tore his mouth away from Cindy and exited the Jeep
in one continuous, savage motion. The driver's door
slammed so hard behind him that Cindy flinched. Hardly
able to believe that she had been kissed with such intensity,
she touched her hot, softly bruised lips with fingertips still
wet from the rain. The moisture she licked up with the tip of
her tongue tasted of more than raindrops. There was passion and hunger, heat and strength.

She tasted of Trace.

The realization made her eyes close as a tremor of hunger and delight radiated through her, changing her body in
the space of a breath, two breaths, dark fire burning.

Rich yellow light flared within the small cabin, then
dimmed as Trace put the glass chimney on the lantern. The
doorway became a golden rectangle that was all but filled by
Trace as he left the cabin. He stepped off the porch and
walked around to the driver's side of the Jeep, heedless of
the warmly falling rain that had dampened his hair and
shoulders. He opened the door, turned the headlights completely off with an impatient flick of his hand and reached
into the back seat. A single suitcase lay there. The suitcase
was Raul's. The contents had been donated by Susan. Trace
grabbed the suitcase as though he expected it to fight back,
yanked it into the rain and slammed the door behind him
again.

Eyes wide, Cindy watched every motion Trace made.
There was none of the air of lazy, sensual humor about him
that he had shown when he had kissed her in the washroom. There had been nothing languid or humorous at all
about the way he had just kissed her. He had wanted her.

And he had trembled with that wanting.

The golden light spilling out of the cabin was eclipsed
twice more as Trace went in, dumped the suitcase on the

door and went back out to the Jeep. He jerked open Cindy's door.

"Out," Trace said flatly.

Cindy opened her mouth.

"For your information, princess, I'm not any happier about wanting you than you are about needing me," he snarled. "So I'd advise you to get your fanny out of the Jeep and into the cabin and do it *now*."

Ten

Cindy was too surprised to speak, much less to move. Before she could gather her wits, Trace leaned in, put one arm under her knees and the other behind her back and lifted her out of the Jeep.

"You're a slow learner, aren't you?" he said roughly.

With no more warning than that, Trace caught Cindy's mouth fiercely beneath his own and tasted the soft depths behind her lips once more. This time his passion didn't catch her by surprise. Her arms slid around his hard neck as she returned the deep kiss with a hunger that equaled his. Trace groaned and his arms tightened until Cindy couldn't breathe. She didn't object. She didn't even notice. Trace was filling her senses to the point that there was no room for anything else. She gloried in the feeling, wanting nothing else, only him.

When Trace finally lifted his mouth he was breathing raggedly, trembling, holding Cindy with bruising strength while warm rain fell over both of them. She made an inarculate sound and turned her face up into the rain, searching blindly for Trace's mouth once more.

"Cindy," he said, then groaned when he saw that light from the doorway had turned the raindrops on her lips into transparent golden gems. "My God, princess, do you know what you're promising me?"

This time Cindy didn't object to being called princess. She knew from the raw need she heard in Trace's voice and saw in his expression that he wasn't baiting her. She whispered his name as she licked raindrops from his chin and the line of his jaw. When the tip of her tongue stroked the corners of his lips, he shivered and made a sound deep in his throat. Her arms tightened around his neck, pulling her closer to his mouth. She was hungry for the heat and taste of his kiss, the sensuous consummation of his tongue mingling with hers while warm rain bathed their bodies.

Cindy didn't know the exact instant when Trace shifted her in his arms, partially releasing her so that her legs and torso flowed down his powerful body. She only knew that suddenly his hands were free to caress the rounded contours of her hips, turning her knees to water, making her as boneless as the falling rain. His long fingers kneaded her buttocks and rocked her against the heated cradle of his thighs, plainly revealing to her the extent of his own arousal.

The honesty of Trace's hunger completely undid Cindy. She had never known anything like it from a man. She gave a husky little cry and moved sinuously against Trace, slowly stroking his body with her own, making the sweet, dark fire within both of them blaze higher. Trace's fingers raked down the back of her thighs, parting them even as he lifted her and held her pressed intimately against the blunt ridge of flesh that was proof of his nearly uncontrollable desire for her. His hips moved once, hard, as though he were plunging into her, and then he moved very deliberately, shaking, listening to her shattered breaths, feeling her tremble wildly as she tried to get even closer to him.

At that instant Trace knew Cindy wanted him as much a
he wanted her—and he was so hungry for her that h
thought he would die of it. He whispered her name agai
and again between hard, deep kisses, wanting all of he
wanting to be sheathed within her satin body until sh
burned out of control, showering both of them with a bla
ing, incandescent release.

But not yet. Not here. Not this instant.

Now that Trace knew Cindy wanted him too much to re
fuse him, he was able to control his own violent need. H
wanted to share much more with her than a fast tumble i
the rain. He needed to know every bit of her skin, to tast
her wild hunger, to absorb her into himself. Only then coul
he begin to ease the raging hunger that had consumed hin
from the first moment he had sensed the untouched woma
smoldering beneath Cindy's aloof exterior.

Reluctantly Trace let Cindy slide down his body until sh
was standing once more on the soft, moss-covered floor o
the cloud forest. She swayed uncertainly, barely able t
support herself. Not understanding why he had let go of her
clinging to his hard, bare forearms for balance, she watche
him with dazed eyes.

"Trace?" Cindy managed to whisper. "Don't yo
want—"

The question ended in a husky cry when Trace's hand
moved over Cindy's rain-slicked blouse, caressing the nip
ples that had hardened into crowns beneath wet, clingin
cloth.

"Oh, yes, I *want*," Trace said, his voice deep and as dark
as Cindy's eyes. "I want you until I'm crazy with it. I wan
things with you I've only imagined before, and I want thing
I've never imagined until right now. You make me wild," he
said, shuddering as he fought to control the passion that wa
burning in the very marrow of his bones, burning throug
the self-discipline he had always taken for granted.

But no more. Through her he had discovered fierce, nearly uncontrollable currents deep within himself, a need to be one with her that was as old as the cloud forest and as new as each breath he took.

Slowly Trace lifted Cindy, bringing her breasts level with his open mouth. With breathtaking care he bit the tip of first one breast and then the other before he returned to the first nipple, drawing it into the hungry, hot depths of his mouth. Wave after wave of sensation burst through Cindy until she felt as though she were dissolving in hot rain, spinning away, burning as invisible streamers of fire seethed through her.

The sound of Cindy's low, broken moan was the sweetest music Trace had ever heard. His fingers caressed her other breast, drawing more of the husky music from Cindy's lips. He lowered her to the ground once more.

Without lifting his mouth from her breast he began unbuttoning her blouse, working up from the taut navel he longed to kiss. When the buttons parted between her full breasts he ran his tongue over her cloth-covered nipple once more before his mouth released her by degrees, biting gently while the whisper of raindrops absorbed her shivering cries.

Finally Trace drew both hands upward from Cindy's waist until they rested in the warm, deep valley between her breasts. Slowly he spread his fingers wide, peeling the wet blouse away from her body until she wore nothing but rain turned golden by the lantern light. Transparent drops fell onto her high, full breasts and gathered on the twin pink crowns.

He had never seen anything to equal her beauty. His hands trembled as he took the warm weight of her onto his palms. With a murmured, reverent word, he sank to his knees and licked the raindrops from her naked breasts.

Cindy saw Trace's lips part, saw the pale flash of his teeth and then felt the piercing sweetness of his mouth cherishing her. Wave after wave of pleasure washed through her, making her sway. Instinctively she braced herself against her

lover's powerful body, holding his head to her breasts with
a primitive, fierce pleasure.

Trace's hands shaped Cindy's spine, her hips, her thighs,
her calves, kneading and caressing repeatedly, sensitizing her
flesh with each sweep of skin over skin. The last time his
hands stroked down the length of her body, every bit of her
clothing came away and pooled around her ankles. The
feeling of warm rain gliding over her skin so intimately was
indescribable. She started to say something, but her breath
and her thoughts scattered when one of Trace's hands slid
up between her legs until he could go no higher.

"Open for me, princess," he whispered, biting gently at
Cindy's breasts and belly, caressing her with his tongue, his
touches as warm and soft as the rain laving her. "I won't
hurt you. I just want to touch you. That's all. Just...touch."

With a stifled cry Cindy kicked free of the clothes that
were swathing her ankles. Then she stood trembling, open
to the rain and to the sensual caresses of the man who knelt
at her feet.

Gently, inevitably, Trace's fingertips combed through the
thick triangle of midnight hair until he could trace Cindy's
layered softness. He cherished her with exquisite care,
memorizing her with repeated gliding touches until he knew
her better than she knew herself. She said a broken word
that could have been his name, but the word was lost in the
husky sound of triumph and need Trace made as he slowly
penetrated the hot secrets of her body. When he could go no
deeper he withdrew as slowly as he had entered, leaving her
empty and trembling.

"Trace," she whispered. "Trace, I..."

Cindy's words became a low moan as his caress took her
slowly once more. She shivered with each movement of his
hand, each tender penetration and gliding withdrawal, tension gathering within her until it burst sweetly, surprising her
even as it drenched her in pleasure. Her trembling legs gave
way. Slowly she sank down onto the moss-clothed ground

until she was kneeling before Trace, bracing herself on his broad shoulders. He smiled darkly and licked the rain from her lips while he stole into her body once more, caressing her, savoring her exquisite softness, absorbing her intimate shivering as her body changed in anticipation of the much deeper sharing to come.

Cindy clung to Trace with her lips and her body while pleasure washed through her to him. He clenched against a tearing shaft of need as he felt her abandoned response to his caresses. He wanted her until it was agony not to take her. He burned to tear off his clothes and sheath himself inside her with a single hot thrust of his body; but despite the repeated, secret rain of her pleasure, she still was so tight to his touch that he was afraid she wasn't ready to accept him.

And he wanted—needed—to be certain of her pleasure. Since they had met she had suffered too much because of his miscalculations. When he finally slid into her clinging heat, there must be no question that whatever cries came from her sweet lips would tell him of ecstasy, not pain.

Trace's hand moved until his thumb could tease the velvet nub hidden within Cindy's softness. Her eyes closed and her head tilted back helplessly as pleasure splintered through her in shivering waves of heat. Her fingers dug into his shoulders and she arched toward him, her body drawn so tightly by need that she couldn't even form the words to tell him that he must take her or she would die.

Trace understood, yet he did not give Cindy what she was crying for. Instead he slid one powerful arm around her waist, supporting her while his caresses took from her the ability to hold herself upright. Eyes half closed, smiling despite his own violent need, he absorbed her sweet cries, wishing he could drink her essence as well, wanting to take her into himself so completely that he would never again feel the emptiness of being separate from her.

After drawing a final, helpless cry from Cindy, Trace caught her mouth beneath his own. Gently he brought her back to herself, stroking her without demand, holding her, kissing her repeatedly, lightly. The heat and taste of him made her sigh with pleasure. Slowly her hands began exploring the broad shoulders and strong arms that had supported her while sweet fire had consumed her. She had never known pleasure such as he had just given to her so unselfishly. She hadn't even known such feelings were possible.

"You're..." Cindy shivered and looked at the golden light and black shadows lying across Trace's face. "There aren't any words," she said huskily. "Masculine. Hot. Powerful. All true, but not the *truth*. I don't know how to describe you except, perhaps, this...."

Slender hands framed Trace's cheeks. Soft lips brushed his mouth again and then again. The moist tip of Cindy's tongue traced the sensitive outline of his lips and dipped hotly into his mouth, withdrawing before he could even react. Her teeth closed lovingly on his lower lip, holding it captive for her caressing tongue. He groaned her name and tightened his arms around her as though to hold her still for the kind of kiss he suddenly, desperately needed. Her fingers spread wide across his chest, but not in an attempt to push him away. She kneaded his flesh with an open appreciation of his hard body that was as exciting as her tongue teasing him.

Hungrily Trace wrapped his fingers around Cindy's head and took all of her mouth, consuming her with deep, hot strokes of his tongue, feeling her instant, utterly honest response. Her hands moved over his chest, tugging at the buttons on his shirt until suddenly it came apart. Her fingers tangled hungrily in the thick, damp mat of hair that she had wanted to touch since the first time she had seen the tempting thatch curling up from his open collar. She could not touch him enough. Biting softly, tugging, tasting, her

hands and mouth roamed over the masculine territory she
had uncovered.

With Cindy's help Trace shrugged his shirt aside, letting
it fall heedlessly to the ground. Her palms slicked across his
wet shoulders and down his arms to his fingertips, then back
up again until her fingers curled into the fine hair beneath
his arms. She made a murmurous sound of pleasure and
stroked gently, savoring the unexpected softness concealed
on such a hard masculine body.

Trace's breath caught and stayed as a thick wedge in his
throat. He hadn't known how sensitive he could be, nor how
arousing it could feel to have a woman slowly, tenderly devouring him. The feel of Cindy's lips and hot tongue nuzzling down his neck, her teeth biting in exciting counterpoint, her breath caressing him in soft bursts of heat—
everything about her open enjoyment of his body set Trace
afire. When her tongue found one of the tight, small nipples hidden beneath his chest hair, he shuddered and
dragged at breath, unable to get enough oxygen to feed the
searing currents of pleasure and hunger coursing through his
body. He tried to stifle a groan when she circled his nipple
with her tongue and then caressed him with the changing
pressures of her mouth. He couldn't bear any more without crying out for her to stop, yet he would have died if she'd
stopped.

"Cindy," Trace said finally, his voice hoarse. "You are
killing me so sweetly...."

In answer her hands kneaded down his muscular torso to
his waist. Turned back by cloth, Cindy's fingers hesitated,
then dipped down inside the waistband. Trace sucked in air
with a soft ripping sound that was echoed an instant later as
his zipper was drawn down by her warm, wet fingers. Her
right hand slid inside his slacks, finding him unerringly,
rubbing over his rigid male flesh with her palm, loving his
heat and the knowledge that it was she who had made him
so swollen and hard.

Trace bit off a curse and a plea as Cindy caressed him,
moaning even as he did. Finally he caught her hand with his
own, trying to stop her, but he couldn't bring himself to remove the sweet pressure of her palm from his throbbing
body. He permitted himself to move his hips once, very
slowly, letting her know his full length, feeling a groan
wrenched from his throat when her fingernails raked lightly,
devastatingly over the cloth that still covered his erect flesh.

"Stop," Trace said hoarsely, moving against Cindy in
frank contradiction of his own command. "Oh, baby,
stop."

"I can't," Cindy admitted, her voice trembling. "Trace,
I've never wanted to touch a man before. I've never
wanted...this."

Cindy's hand eased away from captivity and slid inside
Trace's briefs. The instant their bare skin met, Trace stiffened and shuddered as though lightning were coursing
softly, hotly, wildly through him. He could no more have
prevented the slow surge of his hips as he gave himself to her
than the warm rain could have prevented itself from falling
into the waiting forest.

"Cindy," Trace whispered, holding her hand pressed
tightly against him, trying not to move, failing, wanting to
die of the pleasure her words and touch had given him.
"Cindy, I need you so much I can't even..." His words became a groan as her fingers curled around him, holding him
boldly captive, learning his masculine textures in the same
way he had learned the secret feminine contours of her desire.

"If you want me, take me," Cindy finally murmured,
biting a hard ridge of muscle on Trace's chest.

"Not here. Not now. Not in the rain."

"Yes, here. Now. In the rain." Her lips sucked lightly on
Trace's biceps, his shoulder, his neck, his dark, sexy smile.
She smiled at him in return. "Did you know that rain tastes
like wine when I drink it from your skin?"

Trace's whole body jerked with the lightning stroke of pleasure that raced through him at her words. When she lifted her head he was watching her, his eyes heavy lidded, glittering in the golden light, and she knew that he was going to take her there, right there, with the warm rain bathing their naked bodies.

"Undress me," Trace said almost roughly, biting Cindy's lips, making her moan. He felt her palms on his skin, sliding beneath his briefs, beginning to uncover him. "Wait," he said through clenched teeth, half laughing, half groaning. "If you don't start with my boots, I swear to God I'll still be wearing them when I take you."

Cindy's hands hesitated. She looked up at Trace with hunger and laughter and curiosity in her eyes. "Would you like that?"

Trace smiled down at Cindy as he ran his fingertip over one of her nipples, lifted his hand to his lips and licked up the drops of water he had taken from her tightly drawn crest. "I'd rather be like you, princess, as naked as the rain. But if you want me wearing jungle boots, I sure as hell won't argue the point. I'll take you any way I can get you."

Cindy drew in a deep, ragged breath and brought her hand slowly out of Trace's clothes, caressing him lovingly even in the act of withdrawing her touch. "None of my fantasies involve men wearing jungle boots," she admitted, her voice husky, breathless.

"What do they involve?"

"My fantasies?"

"Yes," he whispered.

"Being wanted for myself. Just me."

"That's all?"

"It's the world, Trace."

"Then I give it you," he said softly against Cindy's lips, kissing her slowly, deeply. "I want you until I can't stand up. You, Cindy. Just you." He bit her lips with tender care, making her shiver and reach hungrily for him. He caught her seeking tongue between his teeth and raked the moist flesh very gently, savoring her tiny whimpers of pleasure. "I want you until it's like dying not to have you. But before I slide into that sweet body of yours, you'll be wanting me in the same way. I swear it."

Slowly Trace released Cindy. He sat and began unlacing his right boot. She went to work on the other one, making little progress because every time she looked up the long length of his legs to his unfastened pants and naked chest her fingers shook so much they were all but useless. After a few moments she simply gave up and stared at him, lost in wondering enjoyment of his powerful body.

When Cindy's hands went completely still, Trace glanced at her, saw her looking at him with frankly sensual approval, and asked himself almost wildly how he was going to keep his hands off her long enough to get undressed.

"Close your eyes, princess," Trace said huskily, kicking off one boot and reaching for the other.

"Why?" she said, startled out of her reverie. "Are you shy?"

"Not likely," he said, his voice caught between laughter and raw passion. "But I'll never get this boot off if you keep looking at me like you can't decide whether I'd taste better with ketchup or mustard. The way you lick your lips is distracting and sexy as hell."

There was an instant of silence before Cindy's laughter rippled in musical counterpart to the rain. Still smiling she closed her eyes and began patting air and raindrops until she found Trace's single booted foot. Getting in the way more than she helped, tangling her fingers with his, she loosened laces until together the two of them managed to tug off Trace's remaining boot. Going only by touch from his naked feet to his clothed knees, her hands worked their warm way up his legs.

"I've never done this with my eyes closed," Cindy said, searching blindly, caressingly, slowly, heading in the general direction of the waistband of Trace's pants. "Or open, either," she added absently, kneading the clenched power of his calves, his thighs, testing the strength and resilience of his muscles. "You're very strong." She heard her own words and laughed softly. "That's like saying rain is wet. Of course rain is wet and Trace Rawlings is strong. It's just that I've never felt . . . and you're so . . ."

Cindy's voice trailed off into the sound of raindrops falling as her hands caressed slowly higher. Somehow Trace had managed to peel his remaining clothes down over his hips while Cindy explored her way up his legs. Now he watched, frozen, while her slender fingers progressed upward toward his naked, rain-slicked flesh. He felt as though he were being drawn on a rack. When he could bear it no longer, he twisted suddenly, kicking free of the last of his clothing.

"Trace?" Cindy asked.

He watched the widening of her eyes, the parting of her lips, and her fingers reaching toward him, trembling. Suddenly she became motionless and looked only at his eyes.

"Trace?" she whispered.

"Whatever you want, princess," he said huskily.

She smiled almost wistfully. "And here I am without a lick of mustard or ketchup," she murmured.

Trace laughed until Cindy's palms stroked all the way up his thighs and her thumbs traced the deep creases where his legs joined his powerful torso. Then his laughter became a hoarse groan. She jerked her hands away.

"Oh, Trace, I'm sorry! I didn't mean to hurt you!"

At first Trace couldn't believe he had heard Cindy correctly. A single look at her downcast face told him that she had meant every word. The memory of her tight satin depths returned to him. Although there had been no virginal barrier to his searching caresses, it was clear to him now that whatever Cindy's past experience with men might have been, it had been long ago and not terribly illuminating.

"You didn't hurt me," Trace said, his voice gentle and rough at the same time. He took Cindy's hands in his own and pulled them back up his thighs. "It just felt so good that I...ahhh," he groaned, "*yes*, like that, just like that...again, princess. Just once more," he groaned, "then...no more, please, no..."

"You're so hot," Cindy whispered, feeling Trace's vitality radiate through her encircling hands as she caressed him wonderingly, savoring his unexpected response, sensing more than the slick heat of rain on her fingers.

Shuddering with pleasure, Trace gently, inexorably freed himself from the sensual captivity of Cindy's hands. Slowly he lifted her until she was astride his thighs. Raindrops and the lantern light falling through the cabin's open door gilded her breasts and the subtle curve of her stomach and made a shimmering mystery of the lush black cloud nestled between her thighs. He tangled his fingers in that cloud slowly, searchingly, rediscovering the depth of her softness and the hot pleasures of her secret, sensual rain. When he finally withdrew she whimpered deep in her throat.

"Did that hurt?" Trace asked, already knowing the answer, wanting Cindy to know it, too.

"Only when you stopped." Cindy's eyes opened and focused on the harshly drawn lines of her lover's face. "Don't stop, Trace," she breathed. Then she saw the rain glistening on his lips and added huskily, "And a kiss...your taste...I love the taste of you."

Trace's hands were trembling when he pulled Cindy down to him. Even as his tongue thrust between her lips, the taut peaks of her breasts rubbed against the mat of hair covering his chest, sending sensations twisting wildly through her. She moaned into his mouth, tasting him, wanting him, shaking with her wanting. When his hand slid between their bodies and captured one nipple, rolling it, tugging on it, she felt fire radiate out from the pit of her stomach. Instinc-

tively her hips moved, caressing him even as she searched for
a way to ease the hungry aching between her legs.

Trace knew what Cindy wanted. He wanted it too, wanted
it the same way she did, shaking with the wanting. Suddenly his palms slicked over her hips and down the back of
her legs. Long, powerful fingers bit sensually into the soft
flesh high on the inside of her thighs, easing them farther
and farther apart while his mouth mated rhythmically with
hers and his tongue promised her pleasures she had never
imagined. With his teasing fingertips he encouraged her to
abandon all hesitation, arousing her until she wept and
opened herself to him and to the hot rain washing over her
violently sensitive skin.

When Cindy felt the first blunt probing of his flesh she
gasped. Trace caressed her slowly, outlining her, learning her
once more, letting her know his own textures, teaching her
that for all his hard strength he could be deliciously smooth,
like satin stretched over throbbing heat. For long moments
he teased her, preparing her with tiny penetrations and
withdrawals until she moaned brokenly and moved her hips,
instinctively trying to capture more of him.

"Easy, princess," Trace said, his voice soft despite the
cruel need that made his body clench as though he were
being tortured. Once again he eased into the outer edges of
her feminine warmth, parting her delicately, withdrawing,
returning. "We're going to take it slowly...sweetly...
slowly...."

"Trace," Cindy said raggedly, shivering, wild for more of
him yet not experienced enough to know how to manage it.
"Now? Like this?"

"Oh, yes. Just like...*this*. You're so tight, so sleek.
Slowly, baby, slow..." Trace groaned against her lips.
"You're beautiful, Cindy...hot...perfect. Don't let me hurt
you," he said raggedly, pressing deeper, feeling her trembling response as though it were his own. "Am I...hurting
you?"

Cindy tried to answer but she could not. The slow consummation was taking her breath, her voice, her mind, her
soul. She tried to tell Trace how exquisite it felt to be filled
so tenderly, so carefully, so completely, but speech was impossible for her. She shivered repeatedly as rings of pleasure expanded up from their joined bodies and burst,
drenching her in sweetness and heat.

Trace felt each hidden quivering of her satin flesh, each
secret rain of pleasure easing his way. The unexpected, deep
intimacy of the sharing took him right up to the edge of his
self-control, wrenching a groan from him, unraveling his
voice and his breath, unraveling him.

"Dark . . . fire," Trace groaned, kissing Cindy between
each word, biting her tenderly, pressing farther into her with
each caress, each word. "So hot . . . so . . . deep. Ahh, love,
I . . ."

And then Trace could say no more. He was fully sheathed
within Cindy, held tightly, completely, and they were sharing every fragmented breath, every soft groan, hot rain
sliding over them, joining their bodies in an incandescent
intimacy that was so intense he didn't know if he would
survive it.

Cindy felt the shudder that took Trace even as he moved
within her. In the wake of his movement, exquisite sensations radiated through her, overwhelming her. She moaned
and moved in instinctive counterpoint to Trace, redoubling
the advance and retreat of his hard flesh within her, crying
softly as ecstasy stole through her again and again, dark fire
blooming, lush flames climbing higher, consuming her until she called out with something close to fear.

Despite his own violent need, Trace heard Cindy and went
utterly still. His hands shook as he threaded his fingers
through her wet hair, lifting her head from his chest until he
could look into her eyes. Her face was streaked with tears
and rain, her eyes were wide, nearly wild, and her mouth

was swollen by the passionate kisses she had given and taken.

"Am I hurting you?" Trace asked, his voice ragged.

Cindy's head moved in a slow negative that made her breasts stir over Trace's hot, wet skin. "It felt so good . . . incredible . . . and then almost . . . frightening."

"Frightening? How?"

"I don't . . . I can't . . ." Her voice frayed. "When you move . . . when I feel you inside me . . ." She shivered and cried out softly as echoes of ecstasy stirred within her, urging her to give herself to her lover once more. "It's the sweetest kind of burning," she whispered, "and I'm being consumed by it, each breath I take, each time you . . ."

"Do this?" Trace asked, measuring himself slowly within Cindy, smiling darkly when she moaned her pleasure.

"Yes," she said shakily, closing her eyes. "Oh, yes, Trace."

"That's how I want you to feel," he whispered, easing his hands from Cindy's hair, finding and caressing her breasts, rubbing her nipples until she moaned and he felt again the melting heat of her pleasure as she tightened around him. "I feel the same way when you move. Look at me, Cindy."

Her eyes opened slowly, heavy lidded and almost wild with a combination of passion and hesitation. "Do you really feel like I do?" she asked.

Trace moved again inside her, retreating and returning with excruciating care, pleasuring both of them until they trembled.

"Yes, I feel it. I'm in you so deep and you take me so perfectly . . . you're in me, too," he said in a gritty voice, sliding into Cindy slowly, feeling her move with him again, wanting to drown in the wild, honeyed rain of her passion. "That's where the sweetness comes, and the fear," he said.

He watched her expression change as ecstasy consumed her softly with each of his motions within her. Seeing his body transforming her excited him almost beyond bearing.

"I've never been this close to anyone before," he said almost roughly, shaking with the restraint he was imposing on himself. "You're burning me so softly, so hotly, it's like dying. Move with me princess. Please. Tell me that it's good for you...." Words died as a low groan was dragged from Trace by the gliding motion of Cindy's hips. "Yes," he said deeply. "Yes, like that. Come with me, love. I need you...with me."

Trace's words and his hands and his heat dissolved all of Cindy's fears. When his fingers closed lovingly around her nipples, tugging at them, hot streamers of sensation overwhelmed her. She arched helplessly into the caress, sliding over him, making both of them cry out with the pleasure they were sharing. Heat welled up within her once more, a shimmering need that could no longer be denied. He thrust deeply into her, taking everything she had to give, giving everything he had in return.

Wonder shivered in Cindy's voice as rapture gently convulsed her, stealing through her body again and again, consuming her. Trace heard the rippling cries of her completion even as he felt the sweet contractions sweeping through her. His own release burst from him, more piercing with each deep pulse, ecstasy pouring through him until he thought there could be no more...yet still the pulses continued through him until he arched like a drawn bow and cried out hoarsely, giving himself to her as he had never given himself to anything, even the hushed mystery of cloud forest and rain.

Eleven

———

Cindy slept long after dawn filled the cabin with a diffuse silver-gold light. She awoke for only an instant when Trace eased from the bed. As soon as he brushed her lips with love words and soft reassurances she slept again. He smiled down at her while he drew the sheet up over her breasts. The temptation to lie down next to her and make love to her in the full light of day was almost overwhelming. All that kept him from giving in were the pale lavender shadows that lay beneath Cindy's eyes, shadows that silently announced her need for more sleep.

Trace lifted his hands carefully from the sheet and turned away from Cindy. He knew if he kept on looking at her, he would touch her. If he touched her, he would make love to her. If he made love to her, he would take her again and again until he lacked the strength even to raise his head, for she was both a wild sweetness in his soul and a dark fire burning in his blood.

Just the thought of joining his body to hers once more made breath hiss between Trace's teeth. Blood pumped through him suddenly, hotly, filling him until he ached. He had never known a lover who suited him half so well. There were so many things he wanted to share with her, so many ways two people could enjoy one another. He wanted them all with her, every one of them, but most of all he wanted to watch her while he pleasured her, to see her skin flush with passion, to taste her, to feel her give herself to him over and over again, sensual fire burning through all inhibitions, all differences, fire burning until nothing remained but two lovers joined all the way to their souls.

If I don't get the hell out of this cabin, I'm going to pull down that sheet and slide into her before she's even awake, before she even knows if she wants me.

And then Trace caught a glimpse of himself in the mirror—stained khaki shirt and pants, beaten-up jungle boots, heavy stubble making his jaw even more square, his dark hair and mustache combed by nothing but sleep and Cindy's fingers. He looked rough, primitive, fully suited to the untamed land surrounding him.

Will my princess want me now, in daylight, when she can see so clearly what a peon her lover is?

Frowning, Trace turned away from the mirror and tried to shake off the feelings of rootlessness and worthlessness that had once defined his life. He and Raul were related, but only because Raul's uncle had felt a sense of responsibility toward a wild American rose whose child probably had not been his. Megan Rawlings had died weeks after giving birth to Trace. Though her passport proclaimed that she had been American, no family could be found in the United States. There was no one to take in the motherless baby.

Finally a priest had picked up Trace and carried him to the Almeda *hacienda*. Once there he had calmly announced that God had answered Esteban Almeda's prayers. A son had been born. Esteban's barren wife had wept, crossed herself

and accepted her husband's purported child into her arms
and her life with the sweetness of a true angel. Yet despite
Maria's love and Esteban's pride in having finally attained
a son, Trace had grown up knowing in his soul that he didn't
belong. He wasn't a true Almeda. The Almedas were the
aristocracy of Ecuador, and he was the bastard child of an
American woman who had had neither family nor husband
to call her own.

Trace had grown up half in the United States and half in
the Andes he loved so well. It had taken him decades of
hard, dangerous living before he had accepted his own
worth as a human being. It had been many years since he
had felt himself less than the equal of any man solely on the
basis of family background or personal wealth.

Yet he felt inadequate today. Cindy had given him so
much, surrendering her fears and herself to him, trusting
him with her lovely, responsive body... and there was
nothing he could give to her in return that wasn't already
hers by birth.

*Cynthia Edwinna Ryan McCall and a man whose only
birthright is a hard body and a skull to match. What a pair
to draw to. It's so funny it hurts.*

Shutting the cabin door softly behind himself, Trace
stepped out into the brilliant mist that permeated and defined the cloud forest. The rain had stopped sometime during the night, leaving behind little evidence of the storm.
Only the places where man had carved out roads or fields
showed the results of last night's rain in swaths of mud and
puddles. The untouched forest took in moisture like an immense, living sponge. Later when the true monsoon rains
came, even the forest's capacity to absorb water would be
exceeded and the rivers would run brown, but for now the
streams were still clear and sweet, gleaming like polished
crystal in the diffuse light.

Trace found a nearly invisible trail leading down into the
huge, steep ravine that lay just beyond the cabin. He had

discovered the twisting, rugged trail years before. It led to a series of waterfalls and pools that were visited only by mist and wild animals. There orchid plants thrived in lush profusion, their extraordinary flowers swaying gracefully in the silence. The orchid garden was a secret place, a hushed landscape where time didn't exist. Trace had gone there often during his wildest years, when he had fought against everything—and himself most of all.

The trail hadn't changed. It was still narrow, easily lost, overgrown, infused with mist. Even so Trace rarely wielded the machete that hung at his belt. He didn't want to make a clear path for any man to use. He wanted the place of orchids and silence to remain as he had found it. Unknown.

He had never taken a single orchid from there, though he knew that even a thousand flowers would not have been missed from the massed magnificence of the ravine's garden. It was simply that there had never been a good enough reason for Trace to make the difficult descent to the hidden river and the arduous ascent out of the ravine simply for a handful of flowers, no matter how rare or beautiful they might be.

But there was a reason now. Down in the ravine's misty silence grew an orchid that had no name, an orchid that had never graced civilized greenhouses or the jeweled breasts of royalty. Of all the orchids Trace had ever seen, that wild orchid was the most superb, as perfectly sensuous and elegant as a pearl. That orchid was something no amount of money could buy, because only Trace knew where the orchid grew, and no amount of money had tempted him to tell of the hidden ravine.

It wasn't money that tempted him now. It was the fact that he had finally found a woman worthy of the orchid's beauty.

The morning was half gone when Cindy woke again. The sound of the cabin door opening and closing curled through her dreams, followed by less definable sounds as Trace took off his boots and clothes and walked to the bedside. Cindy murmured and stirred languidly, reaching for Trace before her eyes were even open, wanting to curl up against him and hear his heart beating beneath her cheek as she had before she slept. When her hands met only tangled sheets, she opened her eyes.

"Trace?"

His name spoken in Cindy's husky voice sent a primitive shiver of sensation down Trace's spine.

"I'm right here, princess."

She turned toward the sound and thought she was still dreaming. Trace's nude body glowed with a sheen of moisture as though oiled. Various textures of hair had been slicked by water until curling patterns were created across his thighs and torso. The muscles she had kneaded with her hands and tested with her teeth were no longer concealed by darkness. He was even more powerful than she had guessed, and so compelling in his masculine beauty that she forgot to breathe.

Trace wanted Cindy with a force that he couldn't conceal, a hunger that made an answering heat uncurl deep in the pit of Cindy's stomach. As she looked at his strength and his arousal, she could scarcely believe how gentle he had been with her last night. He could have overwhelmed her, taken what he wanted and given nothing in return . . . yet he had loved her so tenderly, making her feel as fragile as a virgin, as cherished as a fairy-tale princess.

"But I'm not a princess," Cindy said, her voice soft, her eyes openly approving of everything she saw in the man who stood naked before her.

"You are to me," Trace said simply. Green eyes searched Cindy's face, hardly able to believe the sensuous elegance of silky black hair, porcelain skin, eyes as brilliant as black diamonds and a mouth whose intense pink exactly matched the flushed heart of the orchid cupped in his hands. As

Trace bent down to brush his lips over Cindy's soft mouth, he whispered, "You're too beautiful for a peon, but I want you so much my hands are shaking. Will you make love with me, even though I'm not a prince?"

Cindy's heart turned over at the combination of hunger and hesitation she saw in Trace's haunted green eyes. She reached for him, ignoring the sheet that slipped down to her waist. Slowly she rubbed her fingers over his skin, savoring its satin dampness. He smelled of mist and forest and passion. The combination made her dizzy.

"You're a man," she said huskily, "more man than I've ever known. That's all I care about." A delicate shiver took her as her lips pressed against the taut heat of Trace's navel. "And if I can't hold you inside my body soon, I'll die."

Trace's eyes closed but for a shimmering flash of green as a knife of pleasure and desire turned in his loins. The merest thread of a groan escaped his lips while the tip of Cindy's tongue probed the taut hollow of his navel. When her hands smoothed down his torso, a torrent of desire poured through him, bringing him to his knees beside the bed.

"Cindy, I . . ." he whispered, but no other words could push past the aching closure of his throat when he looked into the midnight clarity of her eyes. He bent his head until he could cherish her lips with his own. When he lifted his head once more, he could speak. Slowly he opened his hands so that she could see what had been cupped protectively within. "I brought this for you."

For an instant Cindy thought that it was a butterfly poised so delicately on Trace's hard palm. Then she inhaled an elusive, fragile fragrance and realized that the graceful curves belonged to the most extraordinary orchid she had ever seen. The satin petals were long and creamy, with the faintest flush of living pink in the veins. In sensuous contrast was the flower's lush fuchsia lip with its elegant frill. At the edge of the frill the pink color darkened until it was nearly black. The balance of color and shape in the orchid was flawless, drawing the eye unerringly toward the throat of the flower, where vibrant fuchsia again slid down the scale of color into a velvety darkness that was just a few shades removed from midnight.

"When I undressed you, I thought of this orchid," Trace said huskily, bending over Cindy, softly pressing her back into the bed until she was half sitting, half reclining against the heaped pillows. "Your breasts are like the orchid's petals, fine textured, creamy, flawless." He bent his head and kissed one of her breasts, catching its tip in his mouth, drawing the sensitive flesh into a tight peak before he released it. "When you're aroused, your lips and nipples are the same color as the orchid's mouth."

The hand holding the orchid came to a rest between Cindy's breasts. "Yes," Trace murmured, comparing the colors. "Like that. Vivid and alive. It's the same here," he said, easing the sheet down until his hand nestled between her legs. "So perfect. Too perfect for a peon. *Princess.*"

"Trace," Cindy whispered, sensing sadness beneath his words, as though he were retreating from her even while his words turned her into honey and sweetly devoured her. "I'm not a princess and I'm far from perfect. My nose is too long and my eyes are too far apart and my figure went out of style a hundred years ago and I've got broken fingernails and scrapes and bruises all over and my hair—" The tumble of words stopped as though cut by a knife. "Trace?" she asked in an aching whisper. "What is it? What's wrong?"

He released the orchid, letting it settle over Cindy's navel as gently as a breath. For the first time he saw the signs left by the cloud forest on her soft body. With gentle fingertips he touched each small shadow bruise, each tiny abrasion, and he cursed himself in searing silence for what he had done to Cindy when he had forced her to march through the cloud forest simply because he hadn't been able to bear the thought of spending another night alone with her and not having her.

And then the night had come, and they had been alone and he had taken her waiting softness and known the beauty of her dark, shimmering fire.

"Does this hurt?" Trace asked, gently picking up Cindy's hand and kissing a slender finger that had a scraped knuckle and a broken fingernail.

"No, it's—"

"Does this?" he interrupted, brushing his lips across a pale bruise on the inside of Cindy's arm.

"No, I—"

"This?" Trace interrupted again, touching his mouth to a small abrasion on her shoulder.

"No, really, I—" Suddenly Cindy's breath sucked in and her thoughts scattered as Trace's tongue gently laved a nearly invisible scrape. Her pent-up breath came out as a sigh when his mouth moved on, leaving her hungry for more.

The tender catechism continued as Trace brushed caresses across Cindy's face and down her other arm, asking at each tiny wound if it hurt, being reassured that it didn't by her half breaths and shivering murmurs of pleasure before he went on to explore other satin territory. Then he came to a faint, rosy mark at the base of her neck and another matching mark between her full breasts.

"Oh, princess, I'm sorry," Trace whispered. "I didn't mean to hurt you."

"You didn't," Cindy said in a husky voice, trembling as his tongue and lips caressed the narrow valley between her breasts.

"Like hell I didn't."

The mattress shifted as Trace flowed onto the bed and knelt over Cindy, looking for other telltale marks of his passion on her creamy skin. She started to object once more that he hadn't hurt her at all, that he had been so gentle despite his own violent need that it still made her heart turn over just to think about it. The words never got past the breath closing her throat when she saw the contrast of Trace's dark stubble and her pale breasts and the sensuous stroking of his tongue over imagined hurts.

"You're so smooth, so gentle," Trace said, caressing her with each word, "and I'm neither. Cindy... Cindy..." His voice caught as he kissed the taut inward curves of her waist. With each caress he looked for and sometimes thought he had found the barest shadows of the previous night, when his mouth and hands had not been smooth enough, gentle enough for the princess who had trusted him. "So perfect," he whispered, caressing the fine-grained skin below her navel with his lips. "I never should have touched you, princess. God knows I tried not to. And God knows I failed."

Cindy tried to reassure Trace, but all she could force past the aching in her throat was an unraveling sigh that was his name. The sight and feel of his face pressed against her abdomen while the tip of his tongue just brushed her skin, caused heat to uncurl in the pit of her stomach, dark fire rippling out through her body, transforming her.

One large hand closed gently around the orchid, caging the flower without moving it. While the tip of his tongue skimmed the orchid's outlines, his other hand gently stroked the silk of Cindy's inner thighs. With tender thoroughness his tongue traced every curve and fold and indentation of the warm orchid held within his circling fingers. He breathed in the flower's exotic essence even as he ravished it so softly that not a mark was left on its lush surface.

"So delicate," Trace said, his voice deep as he sipped at the orchid's exquisite fringe and at the same time stroked his warm palm along Cindy's inner thighs, coming closer to her most sensitive flesh without ever quite caressing it.

When only the center of the orchid remained untouched, his tongue dipped into the soft fuchsia throat until he could taste the fragrant, velvet darkness hidden within the yield-

ing petals. "So lush," he breathed, skimming just once over
Cindy's flushed, aching softness.

Cindy tried to stifle a small sound of pleasure and need,
but Trace heard it. Slowly he looked up into her midnight
eyes. The hand that had caged the orchid during its tender
ravishment opened, leaving the flower nestled in her navel.
Languidly he rubbed the back of both hands against her inner thighs, caressing and teasing her legs farther apart, giving her light touches and skimming promises that made her
breath catch. When at last she lay before him with nothing
between them but the memory of the orchid, he bent down
to her. As his breath flowed across her flushed softness she
gasped.

"Trace?"

"It's all right," Trace said tenderly, his deep voice as caressing as his breath. "You're like the orchid. Perfect. And
like the orchid, you were made for this. This is what I should
have done last night, enjoying you without hurting you,
leaving you...unmarked."

"You didn't hurt me last night. You..." Cindy's breath
tore softly. "What are...ahhh, Trace, you're making me..."

The ragged whimper of pleasure that came from her
trembling lips was all that she could say, the only sound left
to her, and she made it repeatedly while Trace caressed her
as completely as he had the orchid. The knowledge that he
was taking as much pleasure from the intimacy as she was
made the gentle ravishing all the more overwhelming. She
tried to speak, to tell Trace what sweet wildness he was un-
locking within her, but all that came from her lips were rippling cries of passion.

When Cindy moaned and arched against Trace, he fought
against thrusting into her, losing himself in her sultry satin
depths as she was silently, unmistakably demanding that he
do. He wanted that. He wanted it until he felt as though he
were being slowly torn inside out, every nerve on fire, his
blood burning in savage rhythms that matched the violent

hammering of his heart. All that kept him from losing control was an even greater desire; he wanted to bring his trusting princess to shivering completion in his hands. He wanted to know every aspect of her sensual release with all five of his senses unclouded by his own pleasure. He couldn't manage that if he were inside her, for then her sweet fire would burn through his self-control.

When Cindy arched into Trace again, requiring more from him than his relentless delicacy, he shuddered and caged her very carefully in his hands. The words he spoke to her then were unrestrained and elemental in their demands, yet the tenderness of his caresses didn't vary, each touch unraveling her, each word a hushed burning in her responsive flesh, extraordinary sensations radiating up through her body, softly devouring her flesh until only fire remained and she was its center, burning.

Trace shuddered and absorbed Cindy's release with all of his senses, savoring the knowledge that he had given her such intense pleasure. With redoubled tenderness he caressed her, feeling oddly satisfied even as he clenched against his own violent need.

Slowly Cindy opened her eyes, breathing raggedly as echoes of ecstasy rippled through her. She started to speak, but the sight of Trace caressing her so intimately made her tremble. Pleasure burst softly within her once more. In its trembling wake came the knowledge that for all the sweet fire rekindling in her, consuming her, she wanted more. She could hardly believe it, yet she still . . . *needed*.

"Trace."

The husky timbre of Cindy's voice sent a shaft of raw hunger through Trace. He looked up and saw the orchid she was extending to him on the palm of her slender hand. The flower's scent mingled with the heady fragrance of the woman held between his hands. She shivered within his grasp as he caressed the velvet bud of her passion.

"Trace, I . . ."

Breath and words came apart in a shower of heat. When Cindy knew the sultry pleasure of his touch again, she moaned softly and pressed against him, twisting slowly. She felt the shudder that ripped through his powerful body, tightening his hands on her for just an instant.

"Trace," she breathed, reaching for him.

The orchid tumbled softly from her hand to his cheek and then to her thigh. He turned and brushed his lips over the flower before he picked it up and gently set it aside.

"You're more beautiful than any orchid," Trace said, bending to Cindy again.

"So are you," she said, her voice husky with the shivering pleasure that was rising in her once more, seduced from the secret places of her body by Trace's elemental masculine sensuality.

Smiling, Trace turned and kissed the slender fingers that were caressing his cheek. "I'm about as beautiful as that mud hole I finally winched you out of, princess."

"You're wrong," Cindy said, her voice breaking with pleasure at Trace's touch. Looking at him was another kind of pleasure, equally intense. He was utterly male, hard with muscle and brushed with tempting swirls of hair, and the sultry heat of his mouth held her in thrall.

"Trace?"

He made a gently inquiring sound as he caressed her with slow pleasure. Cindy started to speak, then stopped as pleasure shimmered and burst within her. She wanted to tell him what she needed, but the only words she could think of made her blush.

"Trace," she breathed, rubbing her fingers through his hair and being rewarded by a caress that scattered her thoughts. "Come here. I want to whisper..." The words became a moan as he touched her with ravishing delicacy.

Trace closed his eyes and fought a sudden, savage thrust of need at the thought of Cindy's husky voice whispering

sensual demands in his ear while he buried his hungry flesh
in her softness.

"I'd better stay where I am," he said finally. "If you
whisper in my ear, I'll take you slow and deep and hard."

"Yes," Cindy said, sliding down the bed, insinuating
herself beneath Trace, discovering that his skin was as
steamy as hers and that he shook when her hands found the
fascinating combination of satin and pulsing strength that
was quintessentially male. "That's what I want," she said
huskily. "You inside me. Slow and deep and hard. And then
fast, Trace. And hard, very hard."

Cindy's fingertips raked softly, urgently, over Trace's
aroused body, measuring with wonder how much he wanted
her. Even as his breath fragmented into a groan, her fingertips discovered the single sultry drop she had called from his
violent restraint.

"Trace," she said shakily, "take me now." As she spoke
she moved her hips slowly beneath him.

"I'll hurt you, princess," Trace said harshly. "I'm too
big, too rough for you."

"No," Cindy said, kissing his hot skin as she drew him
closer and then closer to her hungry softness. When the
blunt heat of him touched her, she shivered eagerly. "You're
perfect for me. I need you, Trace. Inside me. Filling me."

He felt the truth of her words in the satin flesh that eagerly parted for him. The hot rain of her passion bathed
him, silently begging for a deeper joining. The tangible evidence of her need dissolved his control. His arms swept up
beneath her knees as he pressed slowly against her, into her,
giving her what both of them so desperately wanted, joining them with a slow thoroughness that was a consummation in itself. She made a broken sound as she felt him taking
her, filling her until she overflowed, filling her until she
could take no more.

And then Trace gently lifted Cindy's hips as he slid deeper
and then deeper still, joining himself completely to her,

sealing them one to the other, stopping only when his thighs were cradled against hers and he was fully sheathed within her welcoming fire. Only then did he begin to move, his hips describing slow, sensuous circles against her heated body. She had never felt anything half so intimate, so utterly exquisite. Each time he moved, streamers of glittering pleasure swirled up through her body.

Without realizing it Cindy began to murmur breathlessly, moving in deliberate, sensuous counterpoint to Trace, doubling and redoubling their shared pleasure, until gentle convulsions began to undo her, feeding upon her languidly, sweetly, and she wept with each unraveling ripple of ecstasy. He smiled and rocked slowly in the tight satin cradle of her body as he bent down to sip the tears of ecstasy from her... and still it continued, rocking, shimmering, building and she knew she was going to die of it and she didn't care as long as he was with her, deep inside her, moving, rocking, and flames of pleasure quivering through her, growing, burning.

Cindy called Trace's name as he retreated slowly, unbearably, leaving her empty when she knew she could not live without him. Instinctively her hands slid down to his hips, nails scoring his skin in passionate demand. His breath caught in a deep groan as his whole body clenched. This time he took her in a hard thrust, moving powerfully, restraint slipping away as her nails sank into the flexed muscles of his buttocks at each stroke, nails stinging him sweetly, telling him to withhold nothing of his power.

The urgent caresses inflamed Trace, but not as much as Cindy's husky words shivering against his ear, her body luring him deeper and yet deeper, faster, harder. Her nails scored him with ecstasy, stripping the world away, taking inhibition with it, leaving only the hot pricking of her nails and her passionate words and her fiery softness sheathing him, taking everything he had to give and giving him shattering ecstasy in return.

She caressed him with her hands, her words, her abandoned response, infusing his driving body with more strength, more heat, rapture pulsing from him to her and back again with each breath, each shimmering convulsion deep within her body, and still it was not complete, not enough. He was dying and he couldn't plunge far enough, deep enough, hard enough.

With ancient instinct her hands swept down to cradle and caress the twin sources of his primal need. At the first enfolding touch he thrust into her with a hoarse cry that was her name, abandoning himself to her as completion burst repeatedly from him in an ecstasy that had neither beginning nor end, simply an incandescent pulsing center that was both himself and the woman whose softness called forth and drank the searing pulses of his release.

Racked by ecstasy, Trace held Cindy, knowing that he had touched her soul and she had touched his and nothing would ever be the same again.

Twelve

——

Well, you don't need to look so happy to see me," Susan said in exasperation, put out by Cindy's frankly dismayed expression when she opened the cabin door and saw guests on the doorstep.

Unsuccessfully, Cindy tried not to look guilty. "Of course I'm glad to see you," she said quickly.

"Uh huh. Pull my other leg. It has bells on it."

Raul laughed even as he gave Trace an intent, probing look over Cindy's shoulder. "I would have called, cousin, but you know the difficulty."

"Yeah. The phones are still out, right? Or is it the bridge that's keeping the world at bay?"

Trace's sardonic inflection and smile weren't lost on Raul. Nor was the frank irritation that had come to Trace's expression when he had looked over Cindy's head and seen the other couple standing at the cabin door. Trace had known that his time with his captive princess would inevitably end, but he hadn't known how fiercely he would resent that end when it came.

"Tia would like you to come to dinner," Raul said smoothly. "There might be other guests as well, if the roads are dry enough. If that is the case, there might be unhappiness if you were unable to attend."

Though Raul said no more, Trace got to the bottom line very quickly. The outside world was no longer accepting Raul's radio silence at face value. If communications weren't reestablished at the Almeda *hacienda*, someone from Quito would drive up and "fix" the equipment for them.

That someone would probably be Invers, spurred on by Big Eddy McCall.

Cindy didn't notice Trace's grim expression. She was too busy looking at Susan's daunting physical perfection and remembering how, when Trace had first met Susan, he had looked from Susan to Cindy and then away. Cindy sighed. She didn't measure up to Susan's standard of beauty and she knew it. And even if she tried to forget that unhappy fact, standing around in Susan's clothes—which were a bit loose in the middle and much too tight on top and bottom—was a constant reminder.

Sighing again, Cindy resigned herself to accepting an evening of inevitable comparisons with as much good grace as she could muster.

Trace saw the shuttered look that came to Cindy's face and remembered he had seen that same look once before, when they had first encountered Susan and Raul.

"Cindy?" Trace asked, looking into the enigmatic, crystalline midnight of his lover's eyes. "We don't have to go anywhere if you don't want to."

"It would be best if you did, if only for a few minutes," Raul countered smoothly before Cindy could answer. "While radio reception has been erratic, I suspect that someone is worried about *Señorita* Mc—ah, *Señorita* Ryan."

"You suspect?" Trace asked in a clipped voice.

"Um," Raul agreed. "It is only common sense, is it not? *Señorita* Ryan is a woman alone in a foreign land. Surely her family would be concerned by the fact that she has not been in contact with them for nine days."

"Nine?" Cindy blinked. "Oh, that's impossible. It can't have been that long."

"Forgive me for insisting," Raul said, smiling slightly and giving Trace an amused look, "but it has been closer to ten days than to nine."

Mentally Cindy counted forward from the instant she had left the plane in Quito. First the argument with Trace, then two days on the road, then he had found her and they had slept in the village and then the storm and they had come to the Almeda *hacienda* and then...

Images of Trace splintered suddenly through Cindy's mind. Trace undressing her, loving her with his words, his hands, his mouth, every part of him, and all around them the cloud forest's sensuous rain bathing their interlocked bodies. Trace standing naked before her with an incredible orchid in his hand and sad shadows in his eyes. Trace joining himself with her slowly, deeply, repeatedly, teaching her so many exquisite ways to touch the shimmering ecstasy that waited within.

"We can't have been here six days," she said weakly. "It seems more like two, or maybe three."

Raul just managed not to smile. "I am delighted that you have found your stay with us so pleasant. Especially with Trace as your, ah, host. My cousin tends to regard the cloud forest much more highly than he regards mere men."

"Cindy isn't a man," Susan pointed out reasonably.

"But of course," Raul said, bowing slightly, failing to conceal his smile. "That explains it."

Trace grunted. All that kept him from being outright hostile to Raul was the fact that Cindy had barely looked at the other man—that, plus the clear dismay in her expression when she had opened the cabin door and had seen the end of their timeless days of mutual exploration and passion. The knowledge that Cindy was no more ready to rejoin the world than he was satisfied something deep within Trace, something that he had not even known was there.

"Tell Tia we'll come to the big house for dinner," Trace said in a clipped voice. "It might be nice if you worked very hard on the radio connections between now and then. Even if you can't *receive* messages, you might be able to send them. Try the American embassy, for instance. They have more powerful equipment than most. Tell them Cindy is doing very well, so no one needs to worry about the fact that she's going to stick around the cloud forest until the roads dry out."

Raul's eyebrows climbed. He turned to Cindy. "Is that the message you wish passed on to your family?"

Cindy turned to Trace, whose vital warmth was even now radiating out to her, touching her, enfolding her. His hard hands reached out and gently cradled her face. He bent and brushed his lips over hers once, twice, three times, tasting the warmth of her breath as it rushed out to him in an invisible caress.

"Is that what you want?" Trace whispered too softly to be overheard, touching Cindy's lips with his own between words. "Just ask me and if it's mine to give, it's yours. I promise you, princess. All you have to do is ask. I'll let you go if that's what you want, or I'll keep you here and make love to you in the midst of orchids and rain."

Sudden tears gleamed between Cindy's thick black eyelashes. She stood on tiptoe and pressed her lips against Trace's hungry, sensual, familiar mouth. His arms closed around her with fierce strength. She didn't object to the

possession. She simply closed her eyes and hugged him as
hard as she could in return.

"I told you that *Señorita* Ryan wasn't being held against
her will," Raul said dryly, turning to Susan in the manner
of someone continuing an argument. "Trace may lack a
certain superficial charm at times, but he has more decency
in him than a regiment of polished aristocrats."

Susan's skeptical blue eyes went from Raul to Trace. As
she looked at her friend nestled within Trace's powerful
arms, she sighed. There was no doubt about it. If Cindy was
a captive, she was definitely a willing one.

Susan met Trace's blazing green eyes and said distinctly,
"She doesn't need another Jason."

"You don't know me," Trace said in a cold, flat voice.

"Does Cindy?" Susan retorted.

"Susan, don't," Cindy said quickly. "It's all right. Trace
isn't like Jason. Believe me. You won't have to put me back
together after we... I promise. This is different."

"I hope so," Susan said, touching Cindy's arm. "You
deserve to be loved more than anyone I know." Susan's
smile was both beautiful and very sad as she turned to Raul.
"What is it that you Spanish say? *Que sera, sera.*"

"What will be, will be," murmured Raul. "Yes."

"A primitive point of view," Susan said, looking directly at Trace.

"Don't knock primitive until you've tried it," Cindy said
quietly, looking at Susan. "I've discovered I'm rather
primitive myself. Like my brother. He spent his life looking
for a woman who would want him just for himself. Just a
man called Rye. And then he found Lisa and now he spends
his days looking like a man who has just swallowed the
sun."

Trace heard the complex resonances in Cindy's voice—joy
for her brother, wistfulness, hunger—and knew in that instant why Cindy traveled and lived under a different name.
It wasn't kidnapping she had feared, it was being wanted for

all the wrong reasons. She had hoped to be as lucky as her brother, desired for what he was, not who he was.

"I had given up hoping to find a man who would want me, just me, Cindy Ryan," she continued, pressing her hands over Trace's. "Not my family ties, not any future expectations of wealth or power, nothing but me." Smiling, she brought one of Trace's hard hands up to her mouth. Eyes closed, she kissed his palm and cradled it against her cheek before she said softly, "Now I know how it feels to swallow the sun."

Trace met Raul's enigmatic black glance without flinching while Cindy's words echoed between them. *A man who would want me, just me, Cindy Ryan. Not my family ties... nothing but me.*

Even as Trace's arms tightened around Cindy, he knew he would have to let go of her very soon. There was no hope that she wouldn't find out he had known her real name even before he met her. That kind of secret could never be kept. His only hope was to let her go before she knew the secret. Then, when she learned the truth, she would look back and know that he must have wanted her, just her, for if he had wanted her money he never would have let her go.

When she realized that, she would come to him again in the cloud forest. And he would be there, waiting for her, wanting her with a complex, elemental hunger he had never known before.

"But I'm not going to make Rye's mistake," Cindy continued, turning in Trace's arms, looking at him. "My brother didn't want Lisa to know about his family because he was afraid it would change the way she looked at him. He was afraid she would see money instead of just a man. He didn't trust her, not really, and he almost lost her because of it." Cindy took a deep breath and looked into Trace's shadowed green eyes. "I want you to know that I trust you."

She paused, closed her eyes for an instant and then opened them. When she spoke her voice carried clearly, as though she wanted to be sure that Trace understood every word. "My full name is Cynthia Edwinna Ryan McCall. My father is very... well off."

"Well off," Susan echoed in an amused aside to Raul. "You have heard, perhaps, of 'filthy rich'? That's Big Eddy McCall. Filthy. Rich. Cindy is his one and only daughter."

Cindy searched Trace's eyes, trying to chart any changes the knowledge of her wealth might make between them. Nothing changed, unless it was the bleak twist of pain that showed in Trace's expression the instant before his mouth kicked up at the corner in his familiar, bittersweet smile.

"I always knew you were a princess," Trace said, brushing a kiss across Cindy's upturned face.

"It doesn't matter," she said almost fiercely.

"No. It doesn't matter," Trace said simply. "Not to me. Believe me. *It doesn't matter.*"

Cindy let out a breath she hadn't even been aware of holding. She smiled at Trace, her eyes radiant. She kissed him softly, hardly able to believe her luck. Trace knew who she was and it had changed nothing. The relief was so great she felt almost giddy. She laughed up at him.

"Now that that's taken care of," Cindy said, smiling, "I'm ready to face dinner in Susan's shade."

"Her what?" Trace asked.

"Her shade. You know."

"No, I'm afraid I don't have the faintest idea," Trace admitted, looking perplexed.

"Remember when we first saw Raul and Susan in the Jeep?"

Trace nodded slowly.

"You looked from Susan to me and then you didn't look at me any more." Cindy shrugged. "That's a man's usual reaction. Susan just puts every other woman in the shade."

Hardly able to believe what he was hearing, Trace looked from Cindy to Susan. "Has she always been this blind?" he asked bluntly.

Susan smiled, but there was no laughter in her eyes. "Big Eddy has been buying men to seduce his daughter into founding a dynasty since she turned eighteen. Little wonder she thinks she's not attractive. The men never saw her for the dollar signs in their eyes. That's why she fell like a ripe peach into the hands of the first man who wanted her body rather than her daddy's bank account."

"It's a damned fine body," Trace agreed matter-of-factly, giving Cindy the kind of loving once-over that made her bones melt, "but it's not why I wanted you."

Her eyes widened in dismay.

"There's a dark fire in you that has nothing to do with your body," Trace said, watching Cindy with eyes that reflected that fire. "That's what drew me, what drove me crazy. I would have wanted you if you'd been short, fat and blond. You...burn," he said, running his fingertip over Cindy's full lower lip. "And while Susan isn't bad-looking if you like skinny women..."

"My, how the man gushes," Susan said dryly.

"The reason I looked away after seeing you next to your wise-mouthed friend," Trace continued, ignoring Susan, "was that I felt guilty as hell for what I'd put you through. You were exhausted, wringing wet, muddy, scraped and your clothes were in shreds, and every time I looked at you I wanted to hire three men to beat me for being such an unfeeling bastard as to force-march you through the cloud forest in the first place. So I tried not to look at you. But I failed. Even looking as if you'd been dragged backward through a muddy knothole, you were still more beautiful to me than any other woman ever will be."

Cindy's eyes widened. "Oh," she breathed.

Trace smiled almost sadly, his lips curving so little that his mustache was barely disturbed. He touched Cindy's lower lip again, a caress that was both intimate and oddly withdrawn, as though he were afraid to come closer.

"I hate like hell giving you back to the world, princess," Trace whispered. Then he looked up at Raul. "I'll bring Cindy to the big house before dark."

"Ride over with us. One of the men can drive the Jeep back after—"

"No," Trace interrupted, looking back at Cindy. "I have a few hours left with my princess. I don't want to share them, or her, with anyone."

Without waiting for Raul's response, Trace drew Cindy back into the cabin and shut the door. She looked into his eyes and felt tears burn in her own. Before she could ask a question, the silken brush of Trace's mustache stroked over her lips until they parted on a gasp, permitting the hot glide of his tongue into her soft mouth. He tasted her with aching hunger while he pressed her against himself with slow, powerful sweeps of his hands.

In the space of a kiss Cindy became both pliant and fierce, for she knew that ecstasy waited within the shimmering heat of their joined bodies. And suddenly she couldn't wait for it.

It was the same for Trace, a primal urgency that could not be denied, a stunning foretaste of what it would be to go without the sense of completion that only Cindy had ever brought to him. He groaned and tore open his shirt as her hot mouth slid down his chest. By the time her lips reached his navel he had kicked aside his clothing to stand before her trembling and naked and gleaming with passionate need.

"Love me, Cindy," Trace said hoarsely, reaching for her even as the sultry heat of her mouth bathed him. "Love me as though it were the last time."

Thirteen

Just as Trace drove the Jeep up to the big house, wind blew over the land, making trees bend and ripple like grass. Mist swirled and disappeared, shredded by flashing knives of metallic gold light. Shadows suddenly appeared as sunlight streamed through the cloud forest, making drops of moisture glitter with alien brilliance.

Trace parked next to the Land Rover, turned off the engine and looked over at Cindy with eyes that reflected both the jeweled greens and the deep shadows that surrounded the Jeep. Cindy didn't notice Trace's silent regard; she was lost in the forest's unexpected transformation. He watched her in aching silence. The unveiled light heightened rather than washed out Cindy's colors. Her beauty squeezed Trace's heart in a foretaste of the bitter loneliness that would come when he let his princess go. He reached out to touch her cheek, needing to feel her warmth.

The front door of the big house slammed open and Susan rushed across the screened porch toward the Jeep. Trace's hand fell back to his side before touching Cindy.

"I thought you'd never get here!" Susan said hurriedly, opening the passenger door for Cindy. "Rye has been calling every half hour since Raul patched up enough equipment to get through to the embassy."

"Rye? What does he want? Is something wrong?" Cindy asked as she got out.

"He said it was a 'family matter' and that everyone's fine but that he had to talk with you as soon as possible to make sure things stayed that way. Does that make sense to you?"

"Not—"

"That's a relief," Susan continued, interrupting. "I thought I was the only crazy one around here. Hello, Trace. You look like your usual cheerful self."

Trace gave Susan a sideways glance as he shut the passenger door behind Cindy.

"Brrr. A look like that would freeze sunlight," Susan said in a stage whisper to Cindy. "Do you suppose he'll ever forgive me for thinking that the only way he could keep you at his cabin was if he tied you to a chair? After all, men with dark beard stubble who look and move like jungle predators are hardly likely to inspire confidence in a civilized woman."

Cindy laughed softly. "I've discovered I'm not very civilized, so don't worry about me."

"I'll try, but after Jason..." The sophisticated mask dropped from Susan's face, allowing her worry and love for Cindy to show through. "I didn't think you were going to make it," Susan said frankly.

Before Cindy could say anything, Raul called from the house. "*Señorita* Ryan, your brother wishes to talk to you!"

Cindy looked at the blue sky, sighed, and said, "Guess I'd better find out what Dad's up to now."

"Your father?" Trace asked sharply. "What do you mean?"

"'Family matter' is our code for problems with Dad or our third sibling, who takes after Dad," Cindy called over her shoulder as she ran up the steps to the porch. "Since Mom died, Rye and I sometimes think we're the only reasonably sane people left in the family."

Cindy followed Raul to the radiophone. With impeccable manners he waited until he was sure that she needed nothing more, then shut the door behind her, allowing her all the privacy she might require.

"Hello," Cindy said, picking up the phone. "What is he up to now, and which he is it?"

"Hello, Cinderella. Where the hell have you been?"

Rye's familiar voice made Cindy smile. "I've been enjoying a guided tour of paradise," she said.

"Impossible. Lisa and I own it, remember? It's called McCall's Meadow."

"To each his own paradise. Mine happens to be a cloud forest where mountains and orchids hide."

"Is that where Susan was hiding, too?"

"She wasn't hiding, but she was here. She's fine."

"How about you? Are you fine, too?"

"Never better."

"Thank God. I was afraid that Dad had outmaneuvered you for the second time."

"What do you mean?"

"He's been flying in and out of here like Peter Pan, rubbing his hands and smiling and talking about the grandkids he's going to have from you at last. Seems he's paying some stud called Trace Rawlings a thousand dollars a day to keep an eye on you in Ecuador, and double that if you come home pregnant. Now I know you're a big girl and can take care of..."

Rye's voice began fading in and out oddly, like the light in the room itself. Shakily Cindy groped for the chair that was positioned close to the phone. She sank into the leather cushions and waited to find out if she was going to survive.

"Anyway," Rye's voice continued in Cindy's ear, "I got to thinking about it and was afraid you might be more vulnerable in a foreign country than you would be at home. I didn't want you getting cut up again like you were over that miserable son of..."

Sound faded as Cindy dragged air into her lungs despite the knives of pain twisting inside her body. She barely had the presence of mind to press her palm over the receiver so that Rye wouldn't hear her tearing breath. By the time she had herself under some kind of control again, Rye was beginning to wonder about the lack of input from her end of the conversation.

"Cindy? Yo, sis. You still there?"

Cindy stared at the radiophone. Slowly she reached for the volume control. As she spoke she ran the volume up and down erratically.

"I'm still here, Rye, but the connection is lousy. Can you hear me?"

"I can hear someone fading in and out. Sure as hell doesn't sound like you, though."

"Yes. Well, things are breaking up pretty badly on this end, too. What was that name again?"

"Trace Rawlings. He's some sort of jungle expert according to Dad."

"I can barely hear you." Cindy closed her eyes. "I'm flying out of Ecuador tomorrow. Can I—can I come see you and Lisa for a while?"

"Hell, yes. You're always welcome, sis. You know that. Why do you think I built on the extra suite of rooms after I was married? Lisa loves you as much as I do. She was so excited about having you for a sister that I thought for a while there she would move in with you rather than me."

Cindy gripped the phone so hard that her hand ached as much as her throat. "I love both of you, too," she said as she ran the volume all the way to zero.

Slowly Cindy hung up. She sat in the chair for a long time without moving, not trusting herself to be able to stand, hardly able to think. And then, when she could think, she wished that she hadn't.

How could I have been so wrong about Trace?

The question was painful, but not nearly as agonizing as the knowledge that she had given herself to a man whose body—all of it—was for hire.

Even as Cindy silently screamed that Rye must be wrong, Trace couldn't have made love to her so beautifully if all he had been thinking about was money, she felt herself dying inside. It was Jason all over again, except that Jason had been cruel every inch of the way, making her pay for the fact that his own greed had forced him to pursue a woman he didn't really want.

Trace hadn't been cruel in that way, but the ultimate result was the same. She had trusted herself to a man whose only interest in her was her money. And she had done it twice.

Cindy made a low, choked sound, but no tears came to ease her grief. It was as though Trace had killed even the ability to cry. Yet after Jason had left, she had wept until Susan had been afraid to leave her alone. It would be different with Trace. She couldn't cry for him any more than she had been able to cry at her mother's funeral. She had been a child when her mother had died, and she had felt a child's raw, incoherent sense of betrayal at her mother's absence.

That was how it was with Trace. Cindy loved him as she had never loved anyone. And when that kind of love was betrayed, there weren't enough tears to wash the wound clean, much less to heal it.

"What's wrong, princess?"

Trace's voice came to Cindy as though from an immense distance. Slowly she opened her eyes and looked at the man she had thought was beyond price, only to discover that he was just one more of Big Eddy's greedy recruits after all. Distantly she wished that she could be angry. She wished that she could rage at Trace, releasing the numbing grip of pain on her mind and body. But she could not.

Raging at Trace would be even more stupid than she had already been in trusting him. She needed him for just a bit longer. There were too many miles of rain forest between herself and freedom.

You Tarzan. Me Jane.

But Trace wanted to stay in the cloud forest for a while longer. No big surprise there. He was being paid a thousand dollars a day for his time. Plus the pregnancy bonus, of course.

Cindy closed her eyes and prayed that the numbness would last until she was on the plane out of Quito.

"Cindy?"

She took a deep breath, ignoring the knives sticking into her body, forcing herself to think rationally. If she said she had to leave, Trace would want to know why. There was no way she could tell him. Not yet. Not until she was certain that she could smile and congratulate him on his sexual prowess and then casually walk away from him. She didn't know how long it would be before she attained that level of serenity.

Probably never.

In the meantime she had to get to Quito. She could ask Raul for a driver, but she had seen enough of Raul to know that he wouldn't go against Trace's wishes without a good reason. She doubted that a woman's hurt feelings would even show up on Raul's scale of measuring good reasons.

"Love?" Trace came up to the chair and sat on his heels. Gently he cupped his hand beneath Cindy's chin and lifted her head until she opened her eyes. "Tell me about it. Let me help you."

Cindy looked into Trace's gentle green eyes and found herself believing that he truly cared for her rather than for her father's money. Despite what she knew, despite her past experiences, *she wanted to believe in Trace*. She had no defenses against him even now that she knew what he was.

She was hopelessly in love with him.

The realization panicked Cindy. Ten days ago she would have grabbed the keys to the Land Rover and rushed out of the house and gotten herself stuck in the first bog, where she would have stayed until Trace came along and pulled her out—but not until she first asked for his help. Nicely. And told him why she had been in such a big hurry in the first place.

For a moment Cindy considered trying to buy Trace's cooperation outright, but she knew beyond doubt that he would turn her down flat just the way he had in Quito. Trace did things his way or he didn't do them at all.

She took a deep, careful breath. There was no point in wasting time being more stupid than she already had been. She didn't have the skill or the strength to get herself back to Quito. Trace did. But she couldn't buy his skill. She could only ask for it a few miles down the road when she got stuck on her own—or she could be smart and ask for it right now.

Slowly Cindy's eyes focused on the man she had learned too much about, too late.

"This morning..." Cindy's throat closed.

She cleared it with a sound so tight, so painful, that Trace's eyes narrowed in unconscious empathy.

"You told me...if I wanted something, all I had to do was ask," Cindy continued in a dry voice. "If you could, you would give it to me. That's what you told me, isn't it?"

Trace nodded as he touched her cheek. She flinched subtly at the caress.

"I have to go home," Cindy said starkly. "Will you take me to Quito?"

Trace lifted his hand and looked at her in silence for a few moments. She was far too pale and her eyes were almost wild. Her fingers were clasped together so tightly that her nails were digging into her hands.

"Why?" Trace asked.

"Is that yes or no?"

"Cindy..." His voice died as he looked at her desperately calm face. "Do you really want to leave?"

"Yes."

"When?"

"Now. Right now. This instant. Please, Trace. I'm beg—"

"Don't," Trace said roughly, unable to bear hearing Cindy's pleas. "It's all right, princess," he said, holding her, feeling her lack of response, wondering what had happened, why she was retreating from the cloud forest. From him. "We'll leave right away." His green eyes searched hers. "Can't you tell me what's wrong?"

Cindy closed her eyes and whispered, "Is that the price of a ride to Quito?"

Trace came to his feet in a single savage motion. "We'll be in Quito before noon."

Trace was as good as his word. He took a direct route from the Almeda *hacienda* to the nearest paved road, and from there he drove like a bat fleeing hell. Cindy slept when she could, pretended to be sleeping when she couldn't and said nothing that didn't relate to the necessities of the trip. Trace had little attention to spare from the road in any case. He drove hard and fast, pushing the Rover right to the edge of its mechanical capabilities and holding it there ruthlessly. Driving like that not only made good time, it kept Trace from grabbing Cindy and demanding to know what was wrong. It kept the rage he felt at being cut off from her under control.

And it kept him from asking himself why he felt such turmoil over the end of an affair that was less than ten days old—an affair that he had known must end.

Driving like a bat out of hell didn't, however, keep Trace from sensing at a visceral level that he was somehow the cause of Cindy's pain. There was no other explanation for her distance from him. Assuming he was at the center of her pain, there could be only one reason. Somehow she had found out that he had always known she was Cynthia McCall, not Cindy Ryan.

By the time Trace pulled up in front of Cindy's hotel, he had decided that he was going to put an end to her distance and silence, beginning right then. He shut off the engine and turned toward her. Cindy took one look at his bleak, jungle-green eyes and reached for the door handle. She was too slow. Before her fingers closed around the handle, Trace was holding her in his arms, pinning her back against the seat with his powerful body.

"Since you won't talk to me," Trace said, lowering his mouth to Cindy's, "I'll try another way of communicating with you."

For a few instants Cindy fought against both Trace's superior strength and her own wild desires, but resisting was futile. Her body knew him too well, responded to him too quickly, hungrily reaching for his sensual fire, wanting to burn away the icy grief that was numbing her. With a small, choked cry she stopped fighting against herself, against him, against the need that only Trace had ever been able to arouse and satisfy within her.

When Cindy's lips finally parted for Trace, he sensed the sweetness waiting for him, a sweetness that he needed as much as breath itself. He groaned and took her mouth almost violently, tasting her deeply, wanting something from her that he could not name. When he realized she wasn't fighting him any longer, he tore his mouth away and began sipping tenderly at her eyelids, her cheeks, the corners of her mouth, her lower lip, kissing her so gently that she shivered between his hands, against his body, telling him everything he wanted to know.

"You see, princess?" Trace murmured, nuzzling Cindy's ear, feeling her shiver again, tasting her, biting her with exquisite care. "It doesn't matter that I knew who you were before you came to Quito. After I saw you I would have wanted you if your father was broke and you were wearing rags. Just like it doesn't matter that I'm a peon, a bastard with no real family. You burn when I touch you. I burn when you touch me. That's all that matters. Everything else is just words without meaning."

Cindy's eyes closed as the last flicker of hope that Rye had been wrong was destroyed by Trace's own admission. *I knew who you were the first time I saw you.*

"Cindy?" Trace said huskily, feeling the change in her body, tension draining away, leaving nothing behind. He was holding her but she wasn't there. Not anymore. Not the way she had been, shivering with pleasure at his touch. "Talk to me, princess."

"Thank you for driving me to Quito," Cindy said politely.

"Don't you believe me?" Trace asked, his hands tightening on Cindy's shoulders.

Everything else is just words without meaning.

"Oh, yes," she said softly, opening her eyes. "'Words without meaning.' I believe you. Now, if you'll excuse me...?"

Trace looked at Cindy's fathomless black eyes and felt a chill ripple over his skin.

"Please," she added carefully.

Trace felt a stroke of anguish as he lifted his hands from Cindy's shoulders. He had vowed that he would make Cindy ask him for something, and he had. Twice.

And each time the request had been that he separate himself from her.

"You don't believe me!" Trace said savagely, anger clear in his voice. "You just can't bring yourself to trust a peon, can you?"

Words without meaning.

The only words that mattered were still tolling in Cindy's mind. Trace had known who she was. He had let her make her little speech about trust and had said nothing. Sudden humiliation galvanized her, giving her the strength to leave him.

"I don't know any peons," Cindy said, opening the door.

"You know me," he shot back.

"You're a stud for hire. Studs and peons are two entirely different things."

"What?"

"Big Eddy hired you."

"Your brother was a regular mine of information, wasn't he?" Trace said viciously.

"Did my father hire you?"

"Technically, yes; but what does that—"

The door closed, cutting off Trace's words, leaving him alone in the Rover. He started to get out, then thought better of it. Cindy was angry now. So was he. Much too angry to accomplish anything. It would be better to wait for her to cool down. When she did, she would realize that what they had was too good to throw away just because Big Eddy had been the one to bring them together.

Trace shifted gears angrily and drove away from the hotel, telling himself that he could be patient and understanding about how Cindy felt. From what Susan had said, Cindy had had a rough time with men because of her father. Naturally Cindy would be upset to find out that Trace had always known who she was. But surely it wouldn't take long before she realized that he wasn't some kind of low-life gi-

golo. He had been hired by Big Eddy to keep an eye on h
daughter, period.

When Cindy got past her anger, she would understan
that making love to her hadn't been any part of Trace's dea
with Invers and Big Eddy. If she just slowed down an
thought about it, she would know that the kind of passio
they had shared was one of those things that money simpl
couldn't buy.

Let's face it, Trace told himself. *A man can't fake it i
bed. What he wants—or doesn't want—is right out front fo
anyone to see. Cindy must know that. All she has to do
slow down and think.*

He was still comforting himself with those thoughts whe
Invers knocked on the front door of Trace's apartment tha
night.

"What the hell are you doing here?" Trace asked.

"Delivering mail," Invers said in a resigned voice.

"What?"

"Got some more of that for me?" Invers asked, gestu
ing toward the glass in Trace's hand.

Trace stepped back into the room. Invers followed. A few
moments later he took an eye-watering swallow from th
glass Trace handed over.

"Thanks," Invers said after a moment. "At least I'll di
with the taste of good Scotch in my mouth."

Trace's mouth lifted slightly at the corner, which was a
close as he'd come to a smile since he had walked into Raul'
radio room and seen Cindy looking like the world had bee
jerked out from under her feet.

"Is it that hard to be a mailman in Ecuador?" Trac
asked.

"You know what they used to do with the bearer of ba
news," Invers retorted. He pulled an envelope out of h
breast pocket. "This came to my office by special messer
ger. I'm afraid it's meant for you."

Trace looked down. The envelope bore the name of Cindy's hotel. Written on the outside of the sealed envelope was: "For Stud Rawlings, the best man money can buy."

Trace said several vicious words as he ripped into the envelope.

Invers finished his Scotch in a single swig and muttered, "I was hoping it was a case of mistaken identity. Guess not."

A shower of money spilled from the envelope onto the floor. American bills. Big denominations. Big enough to make Invers suck in his breath hard and fast. Trace didn't even glance at the money, much less try to pick it up. He had eyes only for the message inside.

Big Eddy taught me that a workman is worthy of his hire. The enclosed covers both our original agreement and the days we didn't spend in the cloud forest waiting "for the roads to dry." I've included the pregnancy bonus because if I'm not, it certainly won't be for lack of effort on your part. I doubt that Big Eddy will be so generous but, as you taught me, you never know until you ask.

Too bad I didn't ask the right questions sooner.

The note swiftly became pulp in Trace's powerful hand. He pinned Invers with a savage look.

"*Pregnancy* bonus?" Trace asked with dangerous softness.

A single glance at Trace's grim face made Invers wish himself elsewhere. Immediately. He looked toward the door, wondering if he could make it before he was stopped.

"Not a chance in hell," Trace said succinctly, following Invers's glance. "You're not going anywhere until you tell what you left out when you conned me into getting Big Eddy off your back."

"It's a long story," Invers said.

"So was Scheherazade's. If you're as lucky as she was, you'll survive to finish it."

A long time later Trace sat alone in his apartment, a drink in one hand and thousands of dollars scattered across the floor at his feet. He no longer expected the phone to ring, no longer waited to hear Cindy say that she believed him and wanted to be back in his arms, no longer expected her warmth to fill the aching hollows of his life. She had flown out of Quito hours before, leaving nothing behind but the envelope explaining why she didn't believe in him.

Trace didn't blame her. If he had been Cindy, he would have felt as angry and betrayed as she did.

Wearily Trace leaned his head back against the cushion and thought of all the things that might have been: the woman of his dreams burning in his arms, loving him, and the cloud forest enfolding them. . . .

A draft stirred through the room, whispering over the green bills, herding them across the floor until they gathered around Trace's feet. He didn't notice the money. He never had.

But he didn't expect her to believe that, either.

Fourteen

Autumn had turned the aspen trees into thousands of yellow torches burning against the coming night of winter. Granite peaks thrust against the cloudless blue sky in sawtoothed magnificence. Dark green pines, silver sage and blazing aspens covered the rugged mountain slopes with a living patchwork quilt that stirred beneath a chill, pure wind.

Cindy noticed none of the grandeur of her surroundings as she stood with Lisa and Rye on the porch of their ranch home. In Cindy's soul she was in the center of a cloud forest swathed in mist and orchids and warmth, and Trace's heart was beating slowly beneath her cheek while she slept in his arms.

"Beautiful, isn't it?" Lisa asked, watching the horizon with amethyst eyes.

Rye stood beside her, looking at the woman, not at the land. He smiled with a gentleness that was at odds with his muscular appearance. It was the same for his hand touching his wife. There was a tenderness that was unexpected in a man who looked as rugged as he did. Slowly his finger twined in Lisa's long, almost transparently blond hair which fell in a shimmering cascade to her slender hips. The silken veil was a continuing source of delight to the violet eyed, black-haired daughter who was gurgling serenely in Lisa's arms. Lisa's hair delighted Rye, as well. With open pleasure he stroked a shining tendril between his finger while he smiled at his wife and child.

"The view isn't nearly as gorgeous as you are," he murmured, bending down to kiss Lisa. "And you, too," he added, laughing, when his daughter patted his mouth with her tiny hand.

As Cindy watched the others, she felt a combination of sadness and joy. Lisa and Rye's love for one another welled up invisibly between them, spilling out to enrich everything they touched...and telling Cindy wordlessly just how much she was missing in her own life.

Trace.

Cindy pushed the silent cry into a dark corner of her mind, the same place where she kept the irrational sadness that came every time she realized that she wasn't pregnant. She should have been relieved that there was no legacy of her bittersweet brush with love. But she wasn't relieved. With her period had come a melancholy that could only be lightened by her niece's artless smiles.

The fact that Cindy wasn't pregnant had so depressed her that she had told no one. She was afraid that talking about it would shatter her brittle calm. Besides, as long as her father believed he had been successful, he wouldn't lay any more traps for her.

"Who was that on the phone?" Lisa asked.

"Dad," Rye said, turning reluctantly toward his sister. "Will you call him back?"

Tension tightened every muscle in Cindy's body. "No," she said without looking away from the horizon.

Rye ran a hand through his thick, unruly hair and said, "I don't blame you, sis. If it helps any, when I found out what he'd done, I tore a strip off him wide enough to cover the barn."

"Nothing will change. You know it as well as I do. Nothing either one of us says matters to him. He'll do what he has since mother died—whatever he damned well wants to do."

"What he wants is to talk to you," Rye said bluntly.

"Not really. All he wants to know is if I'm pregnant."

"So tell him."

Cindy fought against the tears welling up inside her, closing her throat. She shook her head in a silent negative and said nothing more. She had refused all calls from her father since she had returned from Ecuador. She had every intention of refusing Big Eddy's calls until she was too old and feeble to pick up a phone.

"He said that Trace Rawlings is on his way to the States," Rye continued. "Dad wants to know if he should pay the pregnancy bonus. If you don't call him, I'll bet he'll be on the first flight out of Texas to here."

For an instant Cindy felt off balance, as though the earth had hesitated in its turning. Then came a slashing disappointment at this further confirmation that Trace was her father's hired stud.

"He can do what he always does," Cindy said after a long moment, her voice as expressionless as her face. "Whatever he pleases."

Lisa looked at Cindy, hesitated, then said quietly, "If you're pregnant, will you stay with us? Please? We want very much to share that time with you. Babies were meant to be shared."

Cindy searched her sister-in-law's unusual eyes and found the same unselfish love there that Rye had discovered during a timeless summer in McCall's Meadow.

"You may have been raised among Stone Age tribes, but you could teach angels how to be kind," Cindy said huskily.

"Kind?" Lisa laughed and kissed her daughter's tiny, waving fist. "More like selfish. I love seeing new life grow, feeling it kick beneath my hands, knowing that someday the miracle will be complete and another person will be standing close to me, talking to me, seeing a world that is both different from and the same as mine. A new mind, a new laugh, a new smile—even new anger and tears. A whole new person to love and be loved."

"Or hurt and be hurt?" Cindy asked painfully.

"Sometimes that's the only path to love," Lisa said, turning to brush her lips over Rye's lean hand. "It was for us."

"And sometimes there's no path to love at all." Cindy's mouth turned down in a sad curve. "We're told that the road to hell is paved with good intentions. I don't think so. I think it's paved with Big Eddy McCall's money."

Cindy stepped off the porch and walked to the beginning of a trail that led to a small creek. She had spent a lot of time by the creek since she had come back to the States. The crystal dance of water reminded her of the many liquid voices of the distant cloud forest where she had loved...and lost.

Rye started after his sister, only to be stopped by a light pressure from Lisa's hand.

"Let the sound of running water and the turning of the seasons heal her if they can," Lisa said. "We can't. We can only love her."

"I would like," Rye said too softly, "to get my hands on this s.o.b. called Trace Rawlings."

"And I would like to help you."

Lisa's smile was as chill as the wind blowing down from the mountain peaks. Rye lifted his wife's small hand to his lips and pressed a kiss into her palm. Other people judged

Lisa by her fragile appearance and spontaneous, radiant smile, forgetting that she had been raised among tribes for whom life was very simple, very direct. Rye never forgot the primitive fires that had forged Lisa's character. She not only loved, but she defended the things she loved with every bit of strength and intelligence she had.

And one of the things Lisa loved was Cindy.

"Too bad we'll never get to meet him," Rye said.

"Yes," Lisa said softly.

She rubbed her cheek against Rye's hand, sending a veil of hair shimmering over her deceptively delicate features.

Trace pulled up in front of the sprawling, recently re-modeled ranch house and shut off the engine of his rented car. There were five vehicles parked in the ranch yard. He wondered which one of them belonged to Big Eddy. The Mercedes, probably. It sure as hell didn't belong on the lumpy dirt road that wound from the state highway to the ranch house.

No one came out to see who had just driven up. Trace lifted a small, hand-size box from the seat before he got out. He mounted the three front steps in a single flowing stride and knocked on the door with more force than finesse. It had been a long flight from Ecuador to Texas, where he had been told that Big Eddy had gone to see his son in Utah. Another airplane had brought Trace to a small airstrip, a rented car and a washboard road leading—he hoped—to Big Eddy.

Trace had dreamed of getting his hands on the man who had cost him the woman of his dreams.

The instant the door opened, Trace knew that the person facing him wasn't his quarry. The man was about Trace's age, slightly smaller in height and build, with the kind of eyes that Trace liked in a man—direct, confident, self-contained.

"Rye McCall?" Trace asked.

Rye nodded.

"I'm looking for Big Eddy."

"You've found him. He expecting you?"

"Yes. But not here."

Rye smiled slightly and moved inside. "Come in out of the wind."

Trace stepped into the house and waited while Rye closed the door behind him.

"Been on the road long?" Rye asked.

"Two days."

Rye's dark eyebrows climbed. "Long drive."

"Only for the pilots. I slept from takeoff to landing both times."

Within Rye, suspicion crystallized into certainty. His gray glance raked up and down the tall, powerfully built man who stood just a few feet away, looking both out of place and quietly dangerous in his worn khakis and jungle boots.

"You're Trace Rawlings."

The shift in Rye's tone didn't escape Trace. He wasn't welcome here. At all.

"Don't worry," Trace said coolly. "My business won't take long."

"You have five minutes."

Rye said nothing more. He didn't have to. Trace knew that he had five minutes to get out of Rye's sight or take the consequences. For an instant Trace wanted nothing more than the violent physical outlet of the fight Rye was offering. Then Trace realized it would solve nothing. It would simply make things worse.

"If you weren't her brother, I'd take you up on it," Trace said calmly. "But she loves you, so hurting you would only hurt her."

Rye met Trace's savage green eyes and knew that Trace meant every word. Curiosity began to compete with anger in Rye. Why should a man like Trace Rawlings care what hurt Cindy? And there was no doubt in Rye's mind that

Cindy was the only thing keeping Trace in check. The subtle change in the way Trace held himself while he waited for Rye's reaction told Rye that the other man was both unafraid of and trained in physical combat.

A motion in the doorway at the far end of the living room made both men turn. Lisa stood there, watching and listening to Trace with the intensity of a wild animal searching for danger. Just beyond her was a half-open door and a partial view of a man sitting behind a desk.

"Are you the man who took Cindy's laughter?" Lisa asked.

Trace's flinch was so subtle that only someone who was watching for just such a reaction would have seen it.

"Yes, I guess I am," he said softly. He looked at the shimmering fall of platinum hair and remembered Cindy's description of her sister-in-law. "You must be Lisa, the woman who makes knives out of glass."

As Lisa nodded, her hair shifted and glistened with ghostly radiance. "Are you here to see—"

"Big Eddy," Rye said quickly, not wanting Trace to know that Cindy was at the ranch.

"About the pregnancy bonus?" Lisa asked.

"I don't know," Rye said before Trace could answer. "He didn't tell me."

"Of course," Lisa said. "It's none of our business, is it? It belongs to Big Eddy and this man and whatever passes for a conscience between them."

"You use those glass knives to cut out men's hearts, don't you?" Trace asked softly as he walked past Lisa to the half-open office door.

"That shouldn't worry you."

Trace hesitated, then gave Lisa a green-eyed glance that concealed none of the shadows within his soul. "You're right. I don't have a heart. I gave mine away. But she didn't want it. I don't blame her. Hearts cause more pain than pleasure."

Before Lisa could speak, Trace walked into the office and stared at the man sitting behind the desk. He was the right size, the right age, and his eyes were a faded gray match for his son's. Big Eddy ignored the interruption. He sat looking off into the distance with an air of melancholy that was almost tangible. His daughter had refused to speak to him.

Trace walked up to the desk, pulled a wad of bills from his hip pocket and dropped the money in front of Cindy's father. The bills slithered across the desk in green disarray.

"What's this?" Big Eddy asked, focusing his shrewd gray eyes on the money.

"A refund. Your money and hers. You can sort it out between you. You're real good with money, I hear. You're hell on people, though. If I'd known you were crazy I'd never have taken the job."

"What job?"

"Guarding your daughter in Ecuador."

"Guarding?" Big Eddy smiled. "Is that what Invers told you? Well, it was true as far as it went."

"It didn't go nearly far enough, did it?"

"But apparently you did," Big Eddy said with real satisfaction. "Is she pregnant?"

Very carefully Trace set down the small box he had been carrying. With a good deal less finesse, he spread his fingers and planted his palms flat on the scarred surface of the wooden desk with enough force to scatter money in all directions. He leaned hard on his hands, hoping that would lessen the temptation to throttle Cindy's father. It didn't.

"Old man," Trace said in a low, rough voice, "you cost me the love of a good woman. If you weren't her father, I'd make you hurt as much as you've hurt me."

There was a sudden movement behind Trace, but he didn't turn away from Big Eddy.

"Love?" the older man asked softly, tasting the word as though it were unfamiliar on his tongue.

Trace's only answer was the predatory violence in his eyes as he watched the older man.

"A good woman loved me once," Big Eddy said quietly. "She died and nothing was ever the same...." He sighed deeply. "We all die, boy. The only thing that goes on is the children of our love, and their children, and their children, world without end. With enough children, she isn't really dead. She's alive. And someday she'll look out at me through the black eyes of my grandchildren or great-grandchildren and she'll smile." He nodded to himself. "Enough children, that's the key. Everyone thinks I want my own name and image out there—Edward McCalls down to the end of time." His mouth curved in a sad smile. "I did, once. No more. I'd rather see her face, young and alive, laughing and loving. Love is all there is that matters in life. The rest is just flash and fertilizer."

For a long moment Trace and Big Eddy looked at one another. Then Trace slowly closed his eyes. When they opened once more, the predatory gleam was gone, leaving behind only emptiness.

"Is there nothing of your dead wife in Cindy?" Trace asked quietly.

Bittersweet pleasure lighted Big Eddy's face. "Cindy is the image of her mother."

"Is that why you don't want her to trust any man enough to marry him?"

"What the hell are you talking about! I've moved heaven and hell to get my daughter married. When that didn't work I settled for pregnant."

"Is that what she wanted?"

"Who?"

"Cindy. Your daughter. Remember her? Or are you so busy thinking about your own dreams and needs that you don't know what you're doing to her?"

"Just who the hell do you think you are to—"

"I'm Trace Rawlings," he said coldly, cutting across Big Eddy's protests. "I'm the man who can take Cindy so far into the cloud forest that the twentieth century isn't even a rumor. And that's just what I'll do if you don't leave her alone. I'll take her away. I swear it. You've ridden long and hard on your solid gold horse, but it's over."

"Do you know how wealthy I am?" asked Big Eddy, more curious than overbearing.

"Do you know what I'd do with your money if I had it?" Trace said coolly. "I'd use it for toilet paper."

Reluctantly Big Eddy smiled. "She said the same thing."

"Your wife?"

"My daughter." He eyed Trace shrewdly. "You really think she'd go with you to that cloud forest?"

"Willingly?" Trace's mouth flattened. "Not a chance, old man. You ruined that for us. But I'd take her just the same. She belongs there. Most people hate the mist, hate the dense forest, hate the wildness. She didn't. So think about it and think hard. Leave her alone or lose her to a cloud forest where all your money doesn't mean one damn thing. Take your pick."

"I should have listened to Invers," Big Eddy said, sighing again. "He told me if you didn't want Cindy, no amount of money would change your mind. And if you did want her, nothing but killing you would stop you from having her."

"One thing would. It has. She doesn't want me."

"Thanks to me?"

"And to me," Trace admitted softly. "We could have survived your meddling. My bungling was different. I didn't believe a princess could love a peon until it was too damn late." Trace watched Big Eddy with opaque green eyes. "Have you decided?"

The older man smiled. "She's all yours, son. I decided that when your friend called and told me that you had shown up at the *hacienda*, that you wanted Cindy and that she wanted you. I was as excited as a kid at a birthday party. She hasn't looked at a man since I bought Jason for her, and that was years ago. I'd given up hope of getting her interested in any man. That's why I picked you. I figured if you wanted her, a determined man like you would find a way past her defenses. And you did, didn't you?''

"Once." Trace looked at his big hands and wondered if he would feel any better after he had had another talk with Invers, who had once again withheld more than he had told. "Are you particularly attached to Invers?"

"Who?"

"My 'friend.' The one who helped you set up Cindy."

"Raul Almeda was the one who helped me. Invers damn near scotched the whole deal. Said if it turned out badly you'd use our butts for a boot rack. Raul had to lean on Invers pretty hard before he'd agree. I still don't know how it went wrong," Big Eddy said, shaking his head. "You know, at first I thought Raul would be the ideal man for my daughter. I suggested it and described Cindy to him. He described you to me. I liked what I heard a whole lot. So I told Raul about Cindy's friend buying cloth in South America, and the rest was so easy, I thought it was meant to be."

Trace hissed a harsh word.

"Well, the logistics of getting you two together and keeping you together were easy enough," Big Eddy amended hastily.

"Was Susan in on it?"

"Hell, no, boy. She'd as soon cut my throat as look at me. But Raul kept his men on her all the way from Quito to the *hacienda*. It went so damned slick." Big Eddy sighed. "Then I had to go and brag to little Eddy and he squeezed Raul's number out of Invers and everything blew to hell and gone."

"Little Eddy?"

"My boy, Rye."

"Cindy would have found out sooner or later. Only dead men keep secrets. Be grateful I wasn't in on the secret sooner, old man. It would have been worth killing to keep."

Trace straightened, retrieved his package and turned to leave in a smooth, continuous motion. As he had expected, Lisa and Rye were standing behind him.

"Relax," Trace said coolly. "I haven't touched a single gray hair on that slippery renegade's head." He hesitated. "Do you know if she's pregnant?"

"Would it matter?"

"She was my woman. If she's pregnant, I want to take care of her. I want the child to be born into my hands...." Trace looked from Rye to Lisa. "But you don't believe me and Cindy doesn't need me, anyway. She has you two." Trace held out the box to Rye. "She left this behind. Will you give it to her after I leave?"

"What makes you think she's here?" Rye asked, taking the box.

"She loves you and you love her," Trace said simply. "If I had been hurt the way Cindy was, I'd go to a place where I was loved."

Trace started to walk around the other two, only to be stopped by a light touch from Lisa's hand.

"Is that where you're going now?" she asked. "To a place where you're loved?"

Trace looked into Lisa's compassionate eyes for a long moment before he said, "I don't have a place like that. I never cared about love until it was too late." He looked at the box in Rye's hand. "When you give that to Cindy, tell her..." Trace's voice faded into silence as he fought for self-control. It was too long in coming. When he spoke, his voice was too husky, almost rough. "I'll always look for her in the mist, even though I know she'll never be there."

Suddenly Trace was moving quickly, brushing past Lisa and Rye, leaving everything behind.

"Wait!" Lisa said.

Trace didn't even hesitate. Lisa ran after him into the living room and caught his arm with surprising strength.

"I want to talk with you. Privately. Please?" Lisa asked, her hand tightening on Trace's arm. "It won't take long. There's a room in the new wing where we won't be bothered. Please, Trace. It's very important."

Trace wanted to refuse but it was impossible. Her soft pleas had sounded too much like Cindy's. Reading his acceptance before he could speak, Lisa smiled gently and took Trace's hand.

Rye waited only long enough to be sure that Trace was listening to Lisa before he turned and walked swiftly through the kitchen and out the back door. He saw Cindy coming from the barn and waved her over.

"Did Dad finally give up and leave?" she asked.

"Not yet, but this came for you." Rye held out the box to Cindy.

She took it with a puzzled look.

"Open it," Rye urged.

Cindy peeled the tape off the top, lifted the lid and gave a broken cry as she saw an incredible orchid that had grown wild in a cloud forest thousands of miles away. A haunting fragrance drifted up from the flower, enveloping her, wrapping her in memories as she had once been wrapped in mist.

There was no note. Nor was there any doubt as to who had sent her the orchid. Gently she lifted the flower from its mossy nest and let the box fall away. Feeling as though she were being torn apart, she bent her head over the orchid while hope and fear warred within her.

"He just wants to know if I'm p-pregnant," Cindy sai
fighting against hope, knowing she wouldn't survive if hop
won only to prove false once more.

"He said, 'I'll always look for her in the mist, ev
though I know she'll never be there.'" Rye looked at t
orchid Cindy was holding and added softly, "His han
were trembling like yours. You can't buy that with mone
sis. Not from a man as hard as Trace Rawlings."

Slowly Cindy lifted her head. Tears shimmered like rai
drops on her cheeks and on the orchid's creamy petals.

"Is he—here?" she asked huskily.

"If I know Lisa, right now Trace is alone in the new de
watching the fire and wondering how in hell she sweet-talk
him into staying when every instinct he has is screaming
him to run back to the cloud forest and lick his wounds
peace."

Before Rye finished speaking, Cindy was running into t
house.

At the sound of the door opening behind him, Tra
turned away with the primitive masculine grace that ha
haunted Cindy's dreams. As she walked toward him she sa
that he looked older, harder, more alone, and his green ey
devoured her with a complex yearning that said more th
words.

"Princess . . . ?" he whispered, afraid to hope.

"I love you," Cindy said, holding out her cupped han
to Trace, within them the orchid trembling as though it we
alive. "I love you."

Slowly Trace cupped his hands beneath Cindy's and be
until he could breathe in the fragrance of both flower a
woman. When he straightened, more clear drops gleam
on the orchid's flawless petals. Very gently he took Cindy
his arms, kissing the tears from her eyelashes, whispering h
love for her again and again. Then he held her close ar

hard, trying to absorb her through his skin into his bones,
feeling tears like warm rain on his cheeks, on hers.

And he knew all the way to his soul that the next time he
looked for her in the cloud forest's swirling mist she would
be there, holding her hands out to him, running to him,
bringing to him the sweet, dark fire of love.

* * * * *

Silhouette Desire

COMING NEXT MONTH

FOUR UNIQUE SERIES
FOR EVERY WOMAN YOU ARE

Silhouette Romance

Love, at its most tender, provocative,
emotional . . . in stories that will make you laugh and
cry while bringing you the magic of falling in love.

6 titles
per month*

Silhouette Special Edition

Sophisticated, substantial and packed with
emotion, these powerful novels of life and love will
capture your imagination and steal your heart.

6 titles
per month*

Silhouette Desire

Open the door to romance and passion. Humorous,
emotional, compelling—yet always a believable
and sensuous story—Silhouette Desire never
fails to deliver on the promise of love.

6 titles
per month*

Silhouette Intimate Moments

Enter a world of excitement, of romance
heightened by suspense, adventure and the
passions every woman dreams of. Let us
sweep you away.

4 titles
per month*